FROST̲BITE 2
LABYRINTH

DAVE JEFFERY

SEVERED PRESS
HOBART TASMANIA

FROSTBITE 2

WWW.SEVEREDPRESS.COM

ISBN: 978-1-922323-96-5

ACKNOWLEDGEMENTS

The creative process is never done in isolation, and this statement is never truer than in the process of telling stories. It is a team of people who bring a writer's tale to life, shaping it and making it ready for you, the reader, to enjoy.

So it is that thanks must go to the team who helped me to put *Frostbite 2: Labyrinth* together. First, to all at Severed Press who support the mayhem contained in the Frostbite series. To Nicola Meaburn, editor of this volume, for making it all make sense. Thanks also to Tom, Shelly and Oscar, beta readers extraordinaire, for telling me where it worked and where it didn't. Finally to my wife, Justine, for her ongoing support and incredible patience.

And, of course, to you, dear reader. Without readers, writers are nothing. Your support is appreciated as always.

Now, it's time to pull on those gloves and turn up the collar. There's a storm on its way …

Dave Jeffery
November 2020

PROLOGUE

Mount Machapuchare, Annapurna Massif, Himalayas

Blasts of frigid wind buffeted the frozen massif, the mountains high above looming from the shadows; grey behemoths ravaged by the storm.

The blizzard turned the two figures moving across the blurred landscape into hazy ghosts. But their determination to press forward, human and yeti crossing the bleached tundra in a quest of pure, unmitigated vengeance, matched the power of the gale.

They forged an unlikely alliance, yet Knowles and Sully had much in common. But the thing that united them most, the glue holding their hotchpotch relationship together, was a common hatred for the creatures they pursued across the Himalayan ice.

As well as alien firepower Knowles had purloined during combat, they both carried emotional baggage, packed by the enemy within the mountain. For Knowles it was a simple case of getting even. Her closest friends had found death on the massif, and it had not come in the form of inhospitable conditions or harsh climate. It had come at the hands of extraterrestrial life, cowardly chameleons who hid in caves and donned yeti fur to masquerade as myth while doling out very real death to those who came across them.

Two of her brothers in arms, two of her dearest friends, slaughtered on the slopes, robbed of both honour and dignity. She was sworn to seek retribution on a grand scale. The hate pulsed through her blood, igniting her body; the artificial yeti pelt, stolen from the alien fraudsters, holding the heat in, keeping the savage cold out.

Behind them was a destroyed alien base, ablaze beneath Mount Machapuchare. A downed Lear jet was buried beneath the avalanche that followed the explosions. In the fire, under the snow, were her friends, collectively known as *The Sebs*, namesakes of St Sebastian, patron Saint of soldiers.

Now *The Sebs* were dead, disbanded, and off mission. Knowles was going it alone, stoked by reprisal, supported by alien hardware and a companion who should equally not have existed.

Sully's fur was caked with snow and dried blood; a fantastic beast, a thing of myth, made real by the brutality of oppression. The aliens had enslaved and destroyed his kin, a process that had taken time - centuries, in fact. His real name was unpronounceable in human tongue, so Knowles improvised and christened him after a Pixar Disney character from Monsters, Inc., a favourite from her childhood. Only this monster was very real and very pissed off. And lugged a huge, granite club which he rested over his broad shoulders.

Shielding Knowles with his mighty body, Sully powered into the gale, head low, fists clenched. His great snout snuffled the brisk air, filtering scent from snow.

"You gettin' anything in that nose of yours, Sully?" Knowles' question was yelled, but her face scarf and the fierce wind made it a small thing.

Sully picked it up regardless. He paused and looked back at her, extending his thickset right arm to the northeast. He followed this up with a low, reverberating growl.

"Okay, we got them on radar," Knowles muttered into her scarf. She hugged the alien rifle to her. "Can't wait to see you again, guys. Gonna have to give you back your hardware, muzzle first and by the end of it, an empty magazine, of course."

As though coming to the aid of their quest, the gale appeared to relent for a few moments, the maelstrom pausing, the clouds overhead separating so they were defined against the grey, featureless sheet that had previously been there.

"Looks like the bitch is about to blow herself out," Knowles said in the sudden silence. But no sooner had she spoken, the plateau was battered by another north-westerly, bringing with it more frenzied snowflakes.

"Guess Mother Nature's still got a score to settle too," Knowles grumbled.

They marched on, but the storm was unforgiving and relentless, the wind slamming into them, pushing and shoving, hampering their progress enough to have Knowles shout out towards the leaden sky in frustration.

"Just back off, bitch! We ain't stopping, you hear me? We ain't fucking gonna stop until every one of those fuckers is dead!"

Sully placed a huge hand on her shoulder. She looked up at him as he gestured to the side of the mountain. Knowles followed his outstretched arm and, through the swirling snow, could just make out a deep fissure in the rock face.

Shelter from the storm. But for Knowles it brought emotional ambiguity.

"We can't take shelter. They'll get away!"

Sully shook his head in defiance. Not in response to her but to her statement. He didn't agree, she realised.

"You sure?"

He confirmed his convictions by tapping his snout and steering his mighty frame towards the rockface, pausing only to urge her to follow him. Another gust almost took her off her feet, reinforcing the sense of Sully's plan.

Despite this, she had to shelve feelings of reluctance in suspending the chase. Still, she had the heat of her rage to keep her warm while they waited out the storm.

They made their way to the fissure, having to dig away snow so that they could enter. The recess went back several feet before a tunnel snaked off into the darkness. Denied access, the wind and snow disappeared as though a switch had been thrown. Now, all that remained was a low maudlin howl as the wind swept past the cave entrance.

Sully and Knowles moved to the farthest wall, where the light was muted but they could see the tunnel was uninhabited. Sitting down, backs against the rugged rock, they leaned into each other, knowing that the storm would soon diminish.

Unlike their thirst for vengeance.

CHAPTER ONE

The helicopter cruised at two-hundred feet above the mountain, low enough for its shimmying silhouette to be seen crawling across the fresh, crisp snowfall below.

The cool air inside the cabin was a cacophony, an aural assault on the four people as they sat on their leather-upholstered benches. Radio chatter rattled through the headphones. Three men, one woman, a single, shared objective.

Search and rescue.

The Leonardo AW189 helicopter was furnished with hi-tech specifications, the floor plan kitted with the absolute best medical equipment money could buy. The interior was a mix of grey leather and smooth plastic. Running the width of the cabin, a central table separated eight seats - four facing each other – as, running either side of the fuselage, quads of bubble windows threw glittering light about the whole space.

The weaponry stowed in the gun racks behind each bench meant that the occupants were prepared to achieve their goal, no matter what the obstacle. No matter what the cost. Their boss determined the parameters - the priority - to order. It was time to honour the contract, and their boss *was* the job.

Professor Marcus Appleby, geologist of renown and infamous entrepreneur.

They'd received the distress call over two hours ago, an acoustic beacon originating from a transponder imbedded in the suits of both Appleby and his wife, Grace. There was no message, just the exacting of a predetermined EVAC protocol. The chopper had scrambled out of Pokhara within ten minutes, covering the forty kilometres to the slopes of Mount Machapuchare in another eight and a half minutes. The rescue, frustrated by the snowstorm that came in from the northeast, forced the chopper off the massif until it abated. The delay had added another forty minutes to their response time.

Now they were no longer against the elements, they were against the clock.

No one knew this more than Commander Chris Havers. His eyes, the colour of rosewood, scanned those opposite him, his hands, gloved and pressed against his headset, large enough to dwarf the cups over his ears.

He'd been in the employ of Appleby Enterprises for over ten years, working his way up from general facility security officer, through tours as a personal bodyguard for the higher echelons of the organisational executive team, until he achieved the dizzy heights as Commander of the CEO Elite Protection Squad.

Unlike many of his staff, Havers had no military background. Instead, he'd carved out a career in the West Mercia Police Force, going from probationary constable to armed police over a twelve-year period. After twenty-five years, and a spate of radical cuts in the force's fiscal budget, Havers found his worldview begin to sour, and the gnawing feeling that the police were fighting a losing battle against the criminal fraternity seemed omnipotent. He walked from his job with thirty years on the clock, determined to focus on a little housing renovation project he'd acquired in Devon.

That idea lasted for two months before Havers started to miss being part of a team. Although, he didn't realise this until a chance meeting in his local pub with Peter Hawkins, an ex-colleague. Over drinks, Hawkins talked about signing up with a new security firm, contracted to Appleby Enterprises. Good money and a sense of purpose beckoned. Havers took the business card Hawkins eventually offered. The next day, he called the number, got the interview, and then the gig. Now it was all about loyalty and duty. Loyalty to Appleby and a duty to find him on the unforgiving slopes below them.

The team that was under his command had been assembled in haste. They were not his regular staff, their capabilities unknown to him, and this made Havers nervous. Appleby had taken the most trustworthy members with him onto the mountain. Havers figured his boss wanted to keep this expedition tight and need-to-know. But, with the mission going south at pace, Havers and his clandestine team were all that was available to mount a rescue without alerting the Nepalese police that someone was on their sacred mountain. Bribery only went so far up the chain and its influence was finite, especially when it came to the region's religious doctrines.

Havers suppressed a sigh. The whole thing fell well short of a coordinated rescue. Yes, they all had paramedic training, but that was the extent of their medical prowess. Anything more serious, they were screwed. But what the fuck else could he do? Duty and loyalty trumped all.

He spoke into his mic. "Collins?"

"Commander?" the pilot said in his ear.

"ETA?"

"Wheels on snow in ten minutes."

Havers scanned the faces about him, each one grim set and focused. It was a team he'd been given but he hoped would deliver. One way or another, he was about to find out.

***

The blizzard had kept Knowles and Sully hunkered in the back of the tunnel for over an hour. Knowles used this time to consider the implications of their mission, what she hoped to gain balanced against what she'd already lost. There was some doubt as to whether her actions were folly, but they came as an irritable itch rather than stinging agony and were easily pushed aside by her resolute mind.

In fact, much of her thinking was shelved, not because it was difficult or poignant, but because Sully had used the opportunity to go to sleep and his jet-engine snores made it hard to think about anything other than beating him to death with a rock.

She chuckled. "We really are the odd couple, big guy. How the fuck did we get here?"

Knowles watched the snow pass by the cave entrance, the wind driving it with enough force to turn it to shadowy streaks. As the wind eased, the flakes began to thin as the quality of light changed outside. A brightness infused the bleached landscape until Knowles had to drag her snow goggles to her eyes to look upon it.

She nudged Sully with her elbow before standing. He came to with a snort, his big eyes immediately alive.

Knowles pointed to the exit. "Come on, Sully. We're leaving."

Peering out on the world, Knowles primed her weapon. The wind had moved on and the whole plateau was silent. Overhead, clouds rolled by, their great underbellies torn open to reveal azure sky beneath.

She kicked her way through the snow that had piled about the entrance, checking that the area was secure. Sully joined her shortly afterwards. As he found freedom from the confines of the cave, he stretched his body and gave out a huge yawn. He finished his ablutions by sneezing snot onto the fresh snow.

Knowles looked up at him. "You're a real catch, you know that?"

He shrugged his shoulders and walked on ahead, Knowles watching him for a few moments before moving out.

Ahead, the snow had been tousled into drifts, creating a valley with smooth, blanched walls. The blizzard had done its worst and the snow,

now up to her thighs, was like walking against the tide of some great, turgid sea.

After a few hundred metres of hard going, Knowles paused and caught her breath.

"Shit," she gasped. "I need to get my ass back to the gym. Blizzard or no blizzard, this is one inhospitable shithole."

Sully grumbled, gesturing to himself and then to the pristine snow.

Knowles nodded as she made a rough interpretation of his hand signals. "Yeah, I know it's your home, my friend. And I *am* tryin' to see it the way you do but … I can't. If you're not cool with that concept, I guess you're gonna have to shoot me."

The hiss of an arc-rifle came seconds later, a streak of orange sizzling across the stark landscape before a plume of steam erupted beside Knowles seconds later, forcing her to dive. As she landed, a second blast went over her head, slicing into the air where she'd been standing only seconds before.

"Shit, that was just a figure of speech!"

She rolled to her left, the snow and ice blurring her goggles as she sought out the sniper. She bumped into Sully who was lying prone beside her, a mound of fur, his great muzzle aimed ahead, great snorts producing mucus and steam.

"Once we nail that fucker, you and me need to have a talk about personal hygiene, fella."

Sully kept his focus ahead, deep brown eyes gazing into the sparse scenery, sweeping for any clue of their assailant's hiding place. The terrain was a blend of exposed, jagged rock and smooth snow, the alien sniper was dug in and well-hidden, the yeti combat-chassis making it the perfect chameleon.

Knowles tried without success to find their assailant. "Gotta get a position on that thing. Any ideas?"

Sully rolled away from her, sending a wave of snow and ice into the air. The response from the rocks to their right was intense, a barrage of arc-bolts cutting into the rising snow, giving Knowles plenty of opportunity to get a fix.

"Well that worked for me," she said as she targeted an area of rock from where the assault originated.

The arc-rifle wasn't a refined weapon, it was more wrecking ball than precision laser. But, for now, it suited her purposes. Her shots hit the outcrop of rocks, the multiple detonations popping like corks in celebration of locating their target. She saw a heap of shaggy fur stagger from the hazing smoke.

Now their assailant was in the open, Knowles was on her feet, the butt of the arc-rifle now rammed into her shoulder, the muzzle - steadfast.

She let go two shots, and the first shattered the right arm, the second tore into the artificial beast's chest, both strikes giving off sparks and flame. The combat chassis toppled backwards and landed heavily, the slippery surface providing no purchase. The body skittered down the slope for a good ten yards before lying still.

"We gotta go check it out, big guy," Knowles called to Sully.

But her companion was already moving, clouds of vapor puffing out of his nose and mouth as he lolloped across the snow. He was midway, and completely exposed, when two more alien yeti machines came into view, their arc-cannons primed.

They opened fire a few seconds later.

CHAPTER TWO

Three members of Havers' rescue team stood as lowly figures, dwarfed against the mottled, rocky precipice to their left as it rose high into the clouded heavens.

The chopper had touched down ten minutes ago, Havers ordering Collins, the pilot, to hold firm until their return. A second team member, Bart Kabumba, was ordered to remain to help Collins protect their ride.

One person moved ahead of the others, an electronic tablet in their hands. They lifted their goggles and peeled back the index finger of the left glove; the digit beneath was sheathed in blue nylon and the fingertip sported a grey, conductive pad so it could be used on the tablet's screen.

Elspeth McCallum stood at 5' 11" and beneath the hood of her parka, her long, red hair was tied into a ponytail. Her ice-blue eyes scanned the tablet, the exposed skin of her cheeks and forehead were so pale, it was almost in competition with the snow at her feet.

Given the bulk of her career had been spent avoiding detection, Elspeth thought it ironic that her green parka and salopettes made her stand out like an iceberg on the River Dee.

She'd been a Mobile Surveillance Officer (MSO) at MI5 for eleven years, joining at the age of twenty-three, two years after leaving university. She'd graduated with a degree in journalism in her hometown of Dundee. Her father – a civil servant - spent long periods of time away from home, an arrangement that seemed to satisfy her mother, a solicitor with her own legal firm.

But the careers of her parents were not for their daughter. Elspeth had designs on becoming a reporter for a national newspaper. This meant humble beginnings with an internship at The Courier, one of the city's local papers. She planned on spending a few years covering local political stories, building enough of a portfolio to submit to the national broadsheets. Her plans didn't involve falling in love, but three months into her internship, that's exactly what happened.

Stewart Thomas was her copy editor. His energetic, yet awkward, persona immediately leaving its mark after their first meeting at the newspaper offices. On her part, it wasn't love at first sight, Stewart's professionalism and his sense of humour were his standout features, and a young Elspeth wasn't looking for a long-term partner, let alone one two inches shorter than her.

But they worked together a lot, and colleagues became friends, and friends became lovers. For most of the next two years they were inseparable, and by the end of her internship, Stewart asked her to marry him. She agreed, of course, setting the date the following year, her dream of working for a large national paper now supplanted by the all-consuming desires of love and life.

The whole thing felt right, as though her life had always been leading up to meeting this incredible man. He was her best friend, her lover, her soulmate. There were people who longed for this kind of love, many thinking it was a work of fiction or some unobtainable romance from the movies. But they were living it, owning each other, happy in such notion, taking comfort from it.

So why the hell did she fuck it all up on a whim, in one fleeting moment of absolute madness?

It was a question she'd asked ever since she'd got drunk on a night out with her girlfriends. The very next morning she'd woken up in bed next to some muscle-bound stranger, who'd never stirred even as she'd got dressed and stole out of his flat, her shame quashing her hangover as she got a taxi back home.

Stewart had been waiting, fraught with worry. Hadn't she seen his messages? Where had she been? He told her he'd almost called the police.

She'd hesitated, thought about telling a lie, say that she'd stayed overnight at one of her girlfriend's houses. But she still had her integrity, even as frayed as it was at that moment in time.

He knew her too well, saw the guilt in her eyes before the tears. The confession had come through great sobs that shook her body as though she was convulsing. Stewart said nothing, but the look on his face was to stay with her forever, the hurt etched into his eyes, the bewilderment. He'd voiced as much.

"But why?" he'd asked.

She could not answer. There was no answer that made it right. Nothing that made sense.

"Aren't you happy?" The desperation to try and understand was heart-breaking.

"Yes." She meant it.

"I thought you loved me."

"I do. Oh, Christ, I do, I'm sorry. So sorry."

He'd nodded, his face inscrutable. Then he'd gone into their bedroom, emerging after a few minutes with a hold-all in his hand.

"I'll be back for my stuff in a few days," he'd said flatly. "When I do, please don't be here."

And with that he walked out of the flat. She never saw him again, he left her everything. The grieving really kicked in from the outset. Months passed, her heart hurt, a physical pain, a tearing that left her lying in her bed at night gasping, but she owned it, embraced it; this was her punishment for betrayal.

She played *Heart and Soul* by T'Pau, over and over. The song was a favourite of Stewart's mother; they were going to have it as the first dance on their wedding day. On one of the few days she ventured out, Elspeth had *Heart and Soul* tattooed on her left forearm. A reminder of what she'd lost.

She sold the flat, moving back in with her parents, and putting the proceeds of the sale into an account, where it remained untouched to this day. The one thing she never attempted was to try to contact him. Partly because further rejection would have cut her like a knife, partly because of the hope he would call her, and if that happened it could only be to reconcile. But it was a fantasy, and time marched on and anaesthetised her raw heart.

One night, over dinner, her father made a suggestion. And that suggestion was MI5.

At first Elspeth laughed so hard she almost choked on a roast potato. Then, her father - a calm, placid man - showed her a recruitment flyer, the contact details in bold black letters.

"So, let's get this straight, Dad," she'd said, "You want me to get over the breakup of my relationship by becoming a spy?"

"I want you to move on. You made a mistake and it's cost you; I understand it. But being around the places you used to go as a couple is like setting fire to the kitchen and then going and sitting in the lounge. How are you able to get through it?"

She'd been bemused by the seriousness on his face. "That still doesn't make sense. Why would you even consider this an option?"

"Because I work for them, darling Daughter."

She'd been stunned but then it made sense, many weeks 'working away', being called away from dinner to take quiet phone calls in his study.

"You work for MI5?" She'd placed her cutlery either side of her plate, the meal forgotten.

"I do. And have for many, many years. It would take nothing for me to help you find something. I know many people."

"I'm not sure I'm cut out for such a thing. I'm still in shock from knowing you're a spy."

Her father had smiled. It was always a polite, supressed thing. "That's more MI6, but I understand your point. There is more to the intelligence service than spying. It's about protecting the country, that same sense of duty you've had for as long as I can remember."

"Maybe I could take a look, do a bit of reading." But his words about duty had paved the way.

In the following days, she was true to her word. She investigated the organisation, explored what types of career were available. The prime motivator was doing something different, taking on the challenge. She knew this would keep her mind focused, protecting it from rumination and melancholy.

As her father had implied, she quickly established that MI5 was not just about agents and subterfuge. There were other roles of interest, and the MSO leapt off the recruitment page based on its diverse nature. It involved gathering intelligence, surveillance of potential threats to national security, and the articulation of said factors. It appealed to her base interest of information gathering and analysis, so she decided to pursue it. But she made an agreement with her father; if she were to get the job, she wanted to do it on her own merits, and he was not to interfere.

Surprisingly, she saw the disappointment in his eyes, a father stopped from undertaking his responsibility for his daughter. But he accepted and said he was there if she needed him.

So, apply she did. Yes, it was with trepidation and a fair amount of scepticism. But as she applied, as she completed the pre-tests and assessments, went for the interviews, and came out with a job offer, things began to take shape.

The focus it took, the sense of achievement, was an uncompromising diversion from her dogged grief, and then it became a mandate by which she joined the institution that was to be her life for the next decade. There were no distractions, no lovers to speak of, just casual acquaintances that fulfilled base needs from time to time. But nothing to which she'd ever deeply commit. Her heart would forever belong to the man she spurned; she knew this because it was true.

Professor Appleby came on MI5's radar when Elspeth had been an MSO for nine years. The brief was clear at the time. Appleby had an unproven reputation as an illicit gem dealer, suspected of funding his vast fortune with the proceeds, as well as international cartel affiliations.

She'd been assigned to shadow Grace Appleby. As head of security for Appleby Enterprises, Grace was a tough nut to crack, but Elspeth was damn good at what she did, and wasn't discovered until three months into the operation. Grace paid her a visit as Elspeth sat in a cafe on her day off. She'd been sipping a cappuccino as Grace slid into her booth and sat opposite, a sweet smile on her face, eyes bright and cold.

"Can I help you?" Elspeth had asked, innocently.

Grace had played with the cuff of her blue, velvet blazer. "No, but I can help you, Elspeth."

Remaining calm, Elspeth had continued the pretence. "I'm sorry. Do I know you?"

"You're good. *Exceptionally* good. So good in fact, I'd like to leave you with this." Grace slipped a brown envelope across the table.

Elspeth's face had been neutral. "I can't accept that."

"You don't know what's in there."

"Makes no difference."

Grace had placed both palms on the table, one each side of the envelope. "Then I'll tell you. It's a contract of employment. Come and work for us. Come and work for *me*."

"I already have a job."

Grace's smile never slipped. "We'll see."

"What's that supposed to mean?"

"MSO's are only of use if they don't get caught, right?" Grace had said, eyes glinting with enjoyment.

"Yet you want to offer me the gig?"

"Like I say, you're exceptionally good. Took us a while to understand what was going on. We could use you."

Elspeth had resisted. "Sorry, you play for the wrong side."

"I've found that right and wrong tend to be an unreliable gauge. Better to think in terms of job satisfaction."

"I love my job." She hadn't been lying.

"I don't doubt that for a second. That's why I'm here offering you a new one," Grace had said, her voice lilting, almost hypnotic. "Same job description, a lot more money, greater promotional opportunities. Just take the envelope. Read the offer, decide. No obligation."

Grace slipped out of the booth leaving the envelope lying in no-man's-land on the table.

"I'll be seeing you, Elspeth."

"Not the most flattering thing to say to a surveillance officer."

Grace giggled. "You really are a gem. TTFN."

So, back in her flat, Elspeth had opened the envelope and found inside a top end, six-figure offer, and the reality that her time in MI5 was coming to an end, whether she took the money or not, became readily apparent. She'd been outed; the MI5 surveillance operation was blown. Appleby's security protocols would come down like a fucking anvil.

Perhaps it was the defiant spark that set her on the path to betrayal all those years ago, perhaps it was the lure of remaining in a job specification to which she was completely passionate, but Elspeth made the decision, and the biggest surprise of all was that it was relatively painless.

The judgment wasn't completely hers, of course. She was no fool; Appleby would have surveillance footage of their café meet and the envelope she'd left behind. Elspeth had ended her MI5 career when she'd taken the A4 slip of manilla and brought it home with her.

There was something deep inside her that surfaced from time to time, the sense of penalty, punishment for deeds that she could not forgive of herself. If she got caught and went to jail maybe that would appease her ongoing, personal debasement. But Grace was true to her word, keeping Elspeth away from nothing but surveillance of those the Applebys considered persons of interest. There was no link to how they were involved or what they needed the information for, it all ended up in a report, for action by those higher up the chain. Plausible deniability in triplicate.

When Elspeth came out to Nepal, to keep an eye on corrupt police officials that would turn a blind eye to Appleby interests as they went to the mountain, the last thing she expected to be was part of a rescue mission. She had rudimentary firearms training as part of her induction, but that was several years ago and the requirement to carry a gun was not in her job description. How the fuck it had got to this was anyone's guess.

Someone had fucked up and, she was pleased to know for sure, it wasn't her. She looked down at her extreme-weather tablet. On the screen a single green dot pulsed on a sea of white and black contours. The dot wasn't stationary, it moved by increments with each pulse.

"What you got, Elspeth?" Chris said beside her.

"The asset device is still active and suggests moving at pace some three kilometres out."

"Just one asset?"

"Difficult to say for definite due to proximity but it appears so. Could be either of them."

Chris knew what his colleague meant. Grace Appleby was in her thirties, military trained and fit as fuck. The Professor also kept in good shape, but could he compete with someone like his younger wife in this harsh climate?

"Matters not who it is," Chris said with a grim tone. "We recover the asset, as per the brief."

He sensed Elspeth's hesitancy. "What is it?"

"If they want to be found, why are they not staying put?"

"Maybe they're seeking shelter in case another storm hits," Chris suggested.

A voice from behind them brought pessimism to the mix. "Maybe they've been taken hostage."

Chris and Elspeth turned to see a tall, bulked-out figure walking towards them, his Parka matted with snow, his SA80A2 assault rifle cradled in his arms. It was Daniel Lake, the third member of their rescue team.

"A ray of sunshine as always, Dan," Elspeth grinned as the big man stopped in front of them.

"I'm not joking," Dan said. He reinforced his words with a scowl.

Elspeth's eyes met his, not blinking. "And I'm not being complimentary."

"Well let's hope there's isn't any fighting going forward," Dan grumbled. "We've brought one dysfunctional and inexperienced unit onto this mountain."

Chris didn't respond to Dan's pointed warning. Instead, he scanned Elspeth's screen one more time and looked up to the path ahead.

"Pull up your zip, Dan. We're moving out."

***

Multiple arc-salvos crackled through the air, the flickering plasma flashes both beautiful and deadly. Snow and rock blasted skywards as a forest of explosions landed, Knowles going low to try and avoid the debris falling all around her.

She looked about, trying to find Sully who, at that precise moment, was nowhere to be seen.

"Sully! A little help here!"

Knowles dived into a drift to her left, putting a mound of snow and ice between her and the oncoming combat-machines. A flash of flame and the hiss of steam followed immediately afterwards, droplets of boiling water smattering her exposed brow.

"Mother-fucker!" she yelled as her cover was eroded by further arc-fire.

A shadow passed over her, and she hit the deck for fear of getting steamrolled. Sully leapt clear with a mighty roar and hurled his club at the nearest pseudo-yeti, the rocky mace striking the creature in the face with frightening accuracy. The head exploded in a spray of sparks and the machine staggered, knocked off-balance by the impact.

Sully bounded over to the decapitated chassis, ducking to avoid a haphazard burst of plasma from the chest cannon as the alien pilot tried frantically to stop his assault. But Sully countered by grabbing a flailing left arm at the bicep. He used his might to swing the machine's bulk towards the second alien machine as though it was his misplaced club, Disorientated, the chest cannon continued firing, taking off the left leg of its comrade, pitching it forwards where it lay incapacitated in the snow.

Sully held onto the arm he'd grabbed and swung the mound of fur in another wide arc, this time sending it spinning backwards. It struck an outcrop of rock with such force the furry exterior ruptured, spilling green slime out onto the floor, great swathes of mist billowing into the air.

Knowles was on her feet in moments, racing to Sully as he reclaimed his club and began beating it down repeatedly on the paraplegic combat chassis, flashes and green fluid splattering the ground, his terrible rage not yet sated.

Knowles moved within his eye line, waving an arm to gain his attention. After a few seconds, Sully rammed the club upright in the snow, leaning against it as he caught his breath.

She looked at the shattered remains at their feet. "I guess there's no word for 'overkill' in your language, buddy."

Knowles squatted; her hands tentative as she explored the bodies. Sully grunted next to her, making her look up to see him shrug and tilt his head, puzzled.

"Just checking how these things work," she explained. "Always best to know your enemy, right?"

Sully sniffed, unimpressed.

"Critic." She chuckled, turning her attention back to assessing their fallen foe.

The fur was a gaudy mix of splattered greens and browns, a combination of alien blood and lubricant. Sully's blows had pretty much obliterated the decapitated machine, the alien pilot nothing more than twisted and broken shell, face battered into a gaping hole through which a thick yellow jelly oozed.

Inside the chassis, Knowles marvelled at the technology surrounding the alien's damaged frame. The walls of the cockpit, located in the upper chest cavity, were smooth and bejewelled with blinking lights of purple and jade. There were intricate switches, slim and made of some metal similar to stainless steel, but with a magenta hue, and the handles had buttons embedded into them, one large and circular, its purpose immediately clear to Knowles: a trigger control for the chest cannon. Below the seating nest were stirrups, where the alien pilot could mimic the walking motions and propel the machine to do its deadly bidding.

Knowles leaned into the chest cavity, reaching in to explore. This earned her a warning grunt from Sully.

"It's okay, partner," she said calmly. "I know what I'm doing."

She moved aside the alien's slender, fractured arm so she could get access to a bank of controls on the back wall. As the arm fell, the elbow struck a row of levers and a sudden high-pitched shriek had both Knowles and Sully clutching their heads in discomfort. Disorientated, they fell away from the chassis, faces contorted with pain.

After a small lifetime, the sonic assault faded, and Knowles was left gasping.

"Man, that sucked."

"Bad noise gone."

"Yeah, and I ain't gonna miss it, fella." Knowles said, rubbing vigorously at her temples.

"Why miss it?"

"It was a joke."

"Joke bad. Like noise."

Knowles turned to face Sully. Realisation had her as dumbfounded as when the penetrating sound had addled her brain. She blinked twice, took a breath, and then spoke.

"I can understand you."

Sully's snout made guttural snorts but, inside her head, Knowles heard words. "I understand too."

"Fucking weird, man."

"Not 'man'," Sully replied. "Better. Stronger."

"Well, you make more sense than most men I've met, that's for sure." She wasn't smiling.

"Bad noise make it happen? Make us understand?"

"I guess so. Let's see what else is inside those things." Knowles moved back to the chassis.

Sully took a few steps backwards. "Not good idea. Last time hurt head."

"I think I preferred it when I couldn't understand a fucking word you said."

"What is the 'fucking' word. You say a lot."

Knowles laughed. "That's for another time, fella."

"Be safe."

He means 'be careful', she thought, warmed with the sentiment.

"Thanks, mate."

Sully scratched his head. "Mate? This same as 'fucking'?"

"Christ," Knowles said, aghast. "There's things getting lost in translation and then there's *that*!"

Knowles decided it best to concentrate on the carcass. In truth, she wasn't exactly sure what she was hoping to find but she was sure that she wanted to end the creatures who had caused both her and Sully so much emotional pain. But first they had to find them, and it was as she thought about this premise, she found herself questioning the sudden appearance of their ambush squad.

"Where the fuck did you come from?" she muttered, scrutinising the locale. "Or, more is the question, where were you headed?"

Forgoing the destroyed machines, Knowles went towards the rocky outcrop, seeking a cave or tunnel entrance nearby. What she found instead was the pool hidden between two large boulders.

It was in the snow, a perfect circle of gelatinous, yellow liquid, that wobbled as though it had a will of its own.

"Hey, come look at this," she called.

Sully sauntered over, using his club as a prop. He looked like a rambler out on a Sunday morning stroll.

As he approached and saw the pool, a frown settled upon his simian features. He looked down into a yellow surface, no more than five feet in diameter.

"Looks like piss puddle."

"Well, I'm not gonna argue on that one," Knowles agreed. "But this isn't a million miles away from what we've seen before."

Sully raised his heavy brows. "Not understand."

"The lagoon."

"The lagoon under mountain. One sunrise walk. Not a million miles."

Knowles sighed. Their newfound ability to communicate was going to need a period of adjustment.

"Okay," she said after some thought. "Yellow lagoon in cave. Same stuff."

Sully recalled the cave beneath the great mountain. It had provided cover as he and Knowles approached the entrance to the alien base they had recently destroyed, taking out a production facility for alien-yeti war machines. It had also been a place where he'd been shot in the shoulder by alien troopers before being captured and subsequently rescued by Knowles.

His recollections had him nodding slowly. "Yes, I remember."

Knowles pointed to the destroyed machines behind them. "So, I think they came from here."

"False yeti comes from underground?"

"Yes."

"We go into earth?" Sully said, not sounding completely convinced.
Knowles nodded.

Sully stepped up and gently moved Knowles aside with incredible ease. "I go first."

"Before you go being all heroic, I have a question."

Sully paused over the hole. "Ask."

"What's your name?"

He gave an awkward grin. "Sully."

"I mean your real name."

His grin remained in place. "You give me real name. I like, I keep."

Knowles nodded. "Okay, Sully. Just be careful, okay?"

His great shape turned and jumped into the pool. Within seconds, as though he'd never existed, Sully was gone.

CHAPTER THREE

Dan Lake searched the landscape about him. The snow plain and rising mountains made him feel small and, despite the urgency of their situation, he took time to relish the omnipotence of nature.

In terms of both upbringing and lifestyle, he was many miles from where he grew up. At 32 years of age, his life had started out on a council estate in the Black Country, Lion Farm Estate to be exact, in a twelve-storey high-rise, that crawled its way free of the tattered urban landscape, the way a thistle powers through faded Tarmac.

His parents were hard working, proud people in low-skilled jobs that paid little. But for Trevor and June Lake, money was not what drove them in life. Their true passion was family and the bonds that came with such a tenet. Being able to work, even though it meant Trevor keeping down three jobs, and June hiring out her services to clean and iron for the more affluent people in nearby Birmingham, meant that the Lakes could at least put food on the table and some vestiges of clothing on the backs of a young Dan and his older sister, Elaine.

As the years went by, the Lakes had another person enter their lives. Dan met Charlie Volk by accident when he was ten years old. It had happened when he'd come in early from playing on the estate, nursing an injured hand after an altercation with one of the many feral kids roaming about the naked streets.

As his mother soothed the cut with *Dettol* and bandages, Dan heard his father talking in the main lounge, and the responses of a soft Scottish accent. Dan had noticed how uncomfortable his mother had appeared when the voice came through the thin walls.

After half an hour of his mother's fussing, Dan said he was going to his room. Passing the lounge on the way, he looked in through the open door and saw a portly, middle aged man with greased back blonde hair and a well-groomed beard.

Charlie had seen him immediately and called him into the room. The first thing Dan had picked up was his father's awkwardness; it was like that of his mother. When he spoke in Charlie's company, Trevor sounded passive, as though he didn't want anyone to hear what was being said.

"I'm guessing this bonnie lad is your Daniel?" Charlie had said warmly, but even back then, Dan could see there was a harshness to the man's eyes. "And what do ye wannae be when ye grow up, laddie?"

Dan had shrugged, making Charlie laugh.

"Maybe you can come and work for me? Good hours, good pay and, if ye pay yer dues on time, no one will give ye any bother. Ain't that right, Pa?"

Dan had seen his father shiver slightly. "Yeah, that's right, Charlie. Sorry, but we've got to get on, got parent's evening at school later."

Given the next parent's evening was over a month away, Dan wasn't sure why his father was choosing to lie. He said nothing more of it, and later, when he was older and knew exactly what Charlie Volk was all about, Dan certainly understood why his father had been so cautious around the guy.

It would be three more years before Dan would see Charlie again, and that day came amongst a time of great sorrow and anger. Dan came to realise that it was in such a climate that Charlie thrived.

Dan's sister, Elaine, was nineteen when she was raped and murdered in an alleyway on the estate. The Lake family were understandably distraught, but their despair turned to rage quickly, and soon Charlie was sitting back on the sofa in their flat, talking in hushed voices, hatching plans for retribution.

But nothing came for free, Dan was to learn later. In their desperation for justice, his parents struck a deal, and that deal involved him. This fact came to light when Charlie came to the flat one cold Sunday afternoon, with photographs he shared with Dan's parents.

His mother had sobbed quietly into her handkerchief, his father merely stared at the presented images on Charlie's smartphone, his face inscrutable.

"Ah, Danny!" Charlie said from the sofa. "These things are not fer you, lad. Not yet. But come yer 18th birthday ye'll be coming to work fer me, and I promise I'll show ye these very pictures."

"What are they?" he'd asked.

"Justice, Danny. Justice."

True to his word, Charlie had given him employment on his eighteenth birthday. And four days into his new job, his new boss had picked him up from home in a red Jaguar car and had indeed shown him the pictures. They featured a man hanging from a lamppost, his body drenched in blood from a slit across his throat. Dan handed the phone back without a word.

"Ye got any questions, son?" Charlie asked as he deleted the images.

"Who is he?"

"The piece of shit that killed yer sister."

Dan was hesitant but already knew the answer to the question he'd asked. He just needed to hear the response. "What happened to him?"

"He paid the price. Yer ma and pa wanted him found and punished. That's what I do. I give voice to the little people."

"Will I have to kill people? For you?" he'd asked tentatively.

"No, son," Charlie smiled.

But, like so many things associated with Charlie Volk, the truth was a nebulous affair.

For the next seven years, Dan worked for Charlie. First, running small errands - taking packages or rucksacks from one place to another, not knowing the contents, and under orders never to look - but, as he got older, becoming involved in the shadowy side of Charlie's business. The transition was subtle, moving from courier to look-out as protection punishments were dealt out on the estate; conducting the beatings himself a few months later.

During this time, another change happened. Dan noticed things in his parents. The more work he did for Charlie, the more he got involved with Charlie's associates (and there were many) yet his parents became more distant. This was a dynamic he could not fathom, and he became somewhat disillusioned. How could it be that he was fulfilling the agreement laid out by his parents and yet they were treating him as though he no longer belonged to them, a cuckoo in the nest, a changeling in his own home?

Over time, this made him resentful, it made him angry.

But the conflict he felt was to be displaced. There was never any chance of him venting it out on his parents. Despite their distance, he loved them, did everything *for* them and the thought of hurting them poured guilt on top of already confused emotions to create a volatile mix. He hated the man who had robbed him of his sister, but he also hated him for being the catalyst for the changes in his life. The confusion and anger festered until, once released, it became uncontrollable.

One night, what was meant to be a beating for non-payment almost became murder when Dan lost it big time. Instead of seeing a repentant client, he only saw the face of the man who had defiled and murdered Elaine. Only the intervention of one of Dan's associates saved the man from irreparable damage, or worse.

Charlie had made things clear as soon as he'd found out. "Get yer act together, son. Punters need to be taught a lesson but there are levels of punishment, ye hear me? Who's gonnae pay for protection if they feel keeping up payments still don't keep them safe?"

At that time, Dan had agreed. He'd meant it but Charlie had spoken to him during a period of calm, when his demons were in an uneasy slumber. Such things were becoming transient, so it was of little surprise to Dan when, three weeks later, another incident left a man dead. His meeting with Charlie was no longer a lesson in restraint, it was an exercise in damage control.

"I got two choices, laddie," Charlie had said. "I either put ye down like the damaged mutt ye are, or I have to cut ye loose from my organisation."

"You'd give me up?" Dan had said bitterly. Though, deep down, he knew he deserved it.

In contrast, Charlie was calm, affirming. "No. Yer're a mess, son. But ye need fucking help. And I don't have the means to give it to ye. Let me be clear, I don't want to kill ye but yer're a liability I'm not prepared to tolerate. So, ye need to do the right thing. Cop for the killing, a fight that went wrong, blame it on what happened to yer sister, how it turned yer head to mush. It'll be manslaughter at the most. Ye'll get the shrinks ye need. And I'll see yer ma and pa right; ye have my word."

It should have felt like a betrayal, but it didn't. For Dan it reinforced the meaning of loyalty to those close to him, his parents, his surrogate family he'd established through working for Charlie.

And when he walked into the local police station and confessed to the killing, he took that belief with him, through processing, through the courts, the trial and ultimately the secure unit where he was sectioned under the Mental Health Act to make sure he received the treatment required to address clearly established Post-Traumatic Stress Disorder and severe grief reactions to the loss of his sister.

In his time spent in the secure unit, he responded well to treatment, took the medication, toed the line. A Section 41 meant that he had regular treatment reviews fed back to the Home Office, as only the Home Secretary could release him from his indefinite sentence.

After five years he was allowed to go into the community unescorted, a year later he was released under a Community Treatment Order (CTO) which meant, in short, if he started to refuse medication or visits from his community nurse, he could be hauled back into hospital.

What he'd gained in insight, he lost in relationships, especially that of his family. His mother died shortly before his twenty-eighth birthday, years of smoking forty a day taking its toll. His father didn't last much longer, grief ravaging him as much as the cancer savaged his wife.

Maybe it was the medication, maybe it was just that he'd been in the frame of mind to cope with such things, but Dan came to terms with the loss of his parents without relapse. Somehow losing family who had lived into their seventies was more acceptable than losing a sister with her whole life ahead of her, and in such heinous circumstances. Dan mourned his kin, taking comfort in the fact he'd re-established a relationship with them before they had passed.

He still carried the guilt of taking a life. That was never to leave him, and he made sure it didn't. There had to be repercussions for such actions, he could not just cast such things aside. He simply wasn't prepared to become without conscience. It would never have happened if he were not undergoing trauma, but that didn't mean it should be forgiven.

The biggest shock came a year after he was discharged from his CTO and working part-time as a driver for a local courier service. The surprise came when one of his deliveries took him back onto Lion Farm estate, and there he saw a familiar red Jaguar, and sitting in the driver's seat was Charlie.

Dan had pulled up alongside Charlie's car, gaining the attention of the older man by beeping the van's horn. Charlie had appeared puzzled, then a great smile came across his face as he gestured for Dan to park up and join him.

Charlie had aged, his businesses now handed over to his cousins, on account of him never having sons of his own. Dan had long since suspected this was why he'd not been on the receiving end of Charlie's gun all those years ago: the guy had unofficially adopted him as his own.

The sour look was still alive and well in his eyes. "Ye're worth more than driving a van, laddie," Charlie had said. "Mind ye, I guess that's how ye started out with me, eh?"

"It's work," Dan had said. "Keeps me busy."

"If ye want work, then maybe I know someone." Charlie's tone was low, secretive.

"I'm out of that kind of thing, Charlie. It's not good for me."

Charlie nodded but continued regardless. "This outfit is different, son. Classy, and most of the time - legit. I've sent them some of my best boys over the years. I've got a good rep with them. And they're always hiring if the people are right."

"Why are you helping me?" It was a question he still asked to this day. Back then it was even more of a mystery.

"Ye always had it in ye to be more than this place. Yer ma and pa knew that, and so do I."

Dan never did buy into Charlie's explanation. The guy was always clandestine, the nature of the business he courted, Dan eventually assumed.

Charlie gave Dan a number to ring. That number was for Appleby Enterprises, and Grace Appleby was his recruiter. Charlie's name got Dan an interview. They already knew his background, all of it. Rather than prove a hinderance, it served as an endorsement, especially supported by Charlie's recommendation.

Since joining the organisation, Dan's belief in loyalty had become further reinforced, the edict was a foundation in Appleby Enterprises. Allegiance was rewarded, devotion a tool for promotion. Just like all the years spent with Charlie, Dan's associates became all he knew, a family, and there was nothing that he wouldn't do to keep his employers safe.

No surprise that this would lead him to becoming part of Appleby's personal security detail for most of his trips abroad. It was only his damn role as security backup that had kept him off the mountain when Appleby had first come up here with Grace and Johns. He didn't doubt Johns' ability, the guy was one of the best security operatives he'd ever worked with, but Dan just wanted to be part of the project.

Instead, like everyone else on the mountain, he was a contingency, never expected to be used. He figured Appleby had his reasons, but it still fucking hurt his pride.

Now he was here, late for the party and left with the stragglers. Tech people and second-rate security staff he could do without right now. Especially the fucking man who was supposed to be in command.

Dan groaned inwardly as Chris sidled up and positioned himself alongside. "You got a few minutes?"

Dan made no attempt to acknowledge his approach. "I'm all ears."

"We're in poor shape here, and I need you to be smart about how we keep our morale." Chris kept his voice low.

"Not getting you," Dan said, staring ahead.

Sighing, Chris stood in front of him. "How about I give you an example of how *not* to do it?"

Dan was nonchalant. "Sure."

Chris' reply was flat. "You know that bullshit attitude earlier with Elspeth? That's how not to do it."

Dan finally looked at Chris, eyes yellowed by his goggles. "We have any problems up here and I can't count on anyone to bring home the boss. Tell me I'm wrong."

"That's admirable, but it's not your responsibility, it's mine."

"So, I'm not wrong?"

Chris remained calm. "You let me worry about the stats, Dan."

"I'm so reassured," Dan mocked.

Chris' reply was soft, non-confrontational. "Look, we're both from the wrong side of the tracks. I was a cop, you weren't. But we're now on the same fucking side, your goals are *my* goals, okay? We've got to work together and get this done. You with me or not?"

"I'm still here listening to your shit, ain't I?"

Chris nodded. It was the best he was going to get, and he knew it.

"Elspeth puts the asset tracker three kilometres out and still moving. We need to pick up pace."

"Okay, boss," Dan said. Without another word, he walked off.

Unimpressed, Chris watched him go. If nothing else, he'd learned one thing for certain, the inhospitable mountain wasn't going to be his only problem on this mission.

***

After a few moments standing at the edge of the pool, Knowles stepped off, and allowed herself to fall into the yellow liquid. Initially, the surface took her weight as though solid, then she slowly sank as though passing through thick jelly. She took a breath as she descended, doing her best to subdue thoughts of drowning.

Her whole body became charged with static, and a great crackling sound filled her ears. Before the sensation became too unbearable, she found herself in a tunnel where rock and blue-alien steel fused together; an amalgam of both terrestrial and extra-terrestrial.

"What the fuck was that?" she breathed as she took in her surroundings.

She looked up, expecting to see the yellow circle above her but instead there was only the solid grey rock of the tunnel roof. Bemused, she sought out her companion.

Sully was a few feet away, checking out the way ahead. The tunnel had an arched roof, smooth metal plates in some places, jagged rock in others.

Knowles cast her eyes down to the floor and saw she was standing on a raised, circular platform, the dull metal grill rattled beneath her boots as she stepped off.

She muttered to herself. "Like most things these days, none of this makes any sense."

Sully's hulking shape approached, the overhead, gaudy spotlights throwing his uneven shadow on the rough ground.

"How's it looking?" she asked, indicating the passageway with a bob of her head.

Sully shrugged. "Long. Lots of rock and shiny stuff."

She smiled. "I'm loving your assessment style. Brief and to the point. People could learn a lot from you."

Sully gave her his trademark puzzled expression, causing her grin to expand. She used the moment to take in her environment and make assessments of her own.

Their sole purpose was to destroy whatever the invaders had built here, or at least get word out to people who had the hardware to do it more effectively. She thought the idea over for a moment. How the fuck was she going to explain this and get someone to believe the incredible events unfolding in these mountains? Let alone find some means to communicate this shit in the first place.

So, you let people know and they believe you. And then what? she thought. *The military arrives, assesses the threat just like Sully assessed the tunnel system, and then comes up with a response scenario. A measured response based on levels of risk, and this threat is off-the-scale and so would be the response. Cave busting cluster bombs aren't sure fire. They'd have to go extreme to neutralise a certain clear and present danger. That would mean nukes. That would mean –*

She couldn't think about such things now. The weight of it almost crushed her, stalling her mind to the point of panic. She sought out the wall, and placed her hand on warm, vibrating steel to steady herself.

"You good?" Sully said in her head.

Grateful for the intervention, she nodded. "Yeah. I'm good."

Sully pointed behind her. "We go that way."

"Why?"

"Bad smell. We find it."

"Shouldn't we be going away from bad smells?"

"We hunt for bad things?" Again, the quizzing expression on his simian features.

"Erm, yes, I guess so."

"Find bad things when follow bad smell. Bad smell *that* way." Sully emphasised their direction with his club.

"Okay, boss," Knowles acquiesced. "Lead the way."

The passageway went east for a good quarter of a mile, a seemingly endless tract of rock and steel, still lit by the eerie purple fluorescents and spot lamps. Within a few hundred yards, Knowles had discarded her polar raiment for fear of passing out with the heat that was being thrown out from the walls. Sully cautioned against casting aside her furs for fear she needed them further on. She gave a reassuring smile; she knew what she was doing, and she knew their chances. Once they got the message topside, there would be so much ordinance dropping from the sky, the last thing they'd be thinking of was the cold climate.

She kept such thoughts to herself, not wanting to worry her companion, if he was capable of such a thing. It struck her, then, that she hadn't known him for that long, a few days at most, and in that time, she had come to trust him like no other. Hell, she'd served on tours in many combat zones, had been part of a small unit of staunch friends and comrades, and Sully was up there with them. An honorary member of *The Sebs*, for sure.

Perhaps it was his strength, perhaps it was the simplicity of his character. He was driven by the purest emotions, she didn't know if he'd show mercy during combat, the rage she had seen him exhibit was terrifying. But she also knew he was deeply loyal to those in his care. And she certainly felt that was the case, that Sully was protecting her the only way he knew how. Had anyone else tried to cosset her, she'd have decked them without hesitation. She was no one's 'girl' and definitely no one's fool. In the end, all Knowles took with her was her rucksack and a determined attitude.

After a while, the tunnel began to open out and a warm breeze came at them. Knowles was reminded of a trip to Crete a few years ago, where she'd stood on the beach, looking out upon the Mediterranean Sea. Thinking of Crete made her think of *Greek mythology* and that of Theseus and the Labyrinth, where the deadly hybrid, Minotaur roamed in the gloomy depths. She pushed such thoughts aside and considered the chamber now before them.

About her, she estimated the cavity was over eighty feet in diameter. There were also breaks in the walls, too regular to be natural, that she recognised as small archways.

"What the hell is this place?" she said.

Sully was silent, standing tall and looking on in awe. For several moments he made no comment and, just when Knowles thought there was an issue, he whispered in his gruff voice.

"Home."

Her response was soft. "What? This is your home?"

"No. *Like* home. A place of my people," he explained.

"Like a village?"

His tongue clumsily sought its way around the word. "Yes. A village."

"And is the bad smell here?"

She watched as Sully took in three great snorts. "Yes. Bad things been here. But also good things."

"Recently?"

Sully nodded.

Knowles gazed at the archways and raised her arc-rifle. "Okay, we'll be cautious. Let's look."

They moved deeper into the chamber.

CHAPTER FOUR

"I feel like a boil on a polar bear's ass," Collins muttered as he sparked up a cigarette. He leaned back against the fuselage of his helicopter and blew out smoke. The engine clicked beneath the overhead cowling and steam rose from the exhaust vents like the ghosts of those lost to the mountain.

"Take a breath. If you can't chill out here, you have no peace in your soul," Bart Kabumba said wistfully.

"Funny." Collins took another drag on his cigarette.

"I mean it. Can't you sense it? This place has purity in its heart. It eases a restless spirit."

Collins bristled with irritation. "I haven't got time for flights of fancy, Bart. I just need to make sure this bird is still able to get off this mountain and fast."

Bart didn't respond, though he knew the pilot had a point. Looking about him, he still couldn't quell the sense of peace that came as he stood before the great mountain of Machapuchare. Yes, there was respect and a sense of insignificance under its shadow, but it was the history - the tradition - that mesmerised him.

The locals called Machapuchare 'fish tail' on account of its twin peaks. They also believed that it was a sacred place, the seat of the Hindu god Shiva, the Destroyer of Worlds. This sacred edict meant that climbers had not been legally allowed on the range for many years. Those found trying an ascent risked deportation and huge fines.

For Bart, folklore and myth were inherent to his own family. His grandmother was known for her healing powers in the small village where his mother was born. It was a far cry from Gulu, the commercial city in Northern Uganda where his parents migrated until President Idi Amin's eight-year reign of terror brought wholesale death and destruction on members of the Acholi tribe, as well as the people of Lango and the Christian communities. In that time over 300,000 people were murdered by fanatical forces and secret police.

30

His mother and father went to the UK in 1978 as refugees fleeing from Amin's brutal regime, settling in the city of Birmingham. They endured the usual knuckle-headed racism ascribed to many migrants, but it was nothing compared to the horror of war and the constant threat of execution. His mother trained to be a nurse in the staff-starved NHS, his father worked on public transport, first a ticket collector on Midland Red buses and then a guard on the rail network.

Alongside a close family network, Bart also had school and college friends who were accepting of him, protected him from taunts and racist chants of others, but were not averse to the insensitive, ill-informed jibes that were masked as 'a joke'. Regardless of this, his determination was to be more than the sum of his parents, that he would make his own way through life and, in doing so, repay his mother and father for the life of relative safety he'd enjoyed.

Things turned bad on his last night at college. He was aware that Emma Brogan, a girl from his geography lectures, was keen on him from his first year at Bournville College, but there was something about her, a coldness, that he found off-putting. His family home had been a place of warmth and affection, but Emma's intentions came with an intense aloofness a young Bart found alien and unsettling.

Fostering new relationships, Bart tried to engage in normal, cordial pleasantries, a joke or two, his gentle demeanour attracting a small group of likeminded friends. Emma was always on the fringes, her awkward nature pushing her away from the rest of the group, making Bart feel bad for her to the point where he was more inclusive than he perhaps should have been. He'd chat with her and she would respond with a disproportionately loud and coquettish laugh, and he put this down as compensation for her shyness.

His experience with women was beyond poor, his focus was on getting good grades and getting a respectable job to support his family in the future. And, as time went on, other behaviours became apparent. But Emma's actions were subtle: lingering fingers on the shoulder, for instance, or a fleeting palm on his thigh or knee. Nothing of substance, nothing definitive, an ever-present room for doubt.

Until she day she tried to kiss him.

It had happened on a study session at college. Bart's study group had called it a day and after a few token exchanges decided to head off home. Checking his watch, Bart noted there was still twenty minutes until his bus was due to depart. As he packed away his things, he felt a presence, and, when he looked up, saw Emma still sitting across from him. Her stare was intense, the faint hint of a smile on her lips unnerving him.

She widened her smile. "I like you."

"Sorry?"

Emma got up and tentatively walked over to him, stood over him. And then stooped and tried to kiss him. He avoided her lips by pretending to reach down for something in his rucksack, tainting the moment, making her step back.

He gave the impression he'd not realised her intention and bid her a farewell, heading out to the bus stop, heart pounding.

In the second year, Bart made sure he sat away from Emma in lectures, avoiding any opportunity for her to corner him. He arranged to meet his friends off campus, feeling bad about Emma's exclusion, but the thought of another one of her affectionate ambushes seemed even worse. Once the core content of the course had been delivered, Bart used chunks of study time to stay away from college, going in just to submit sample essays to his tutors, or have telephone discussions with them to make sure he was on track.

He stayed in touch with his friends, too – meeting them for evenings outside college, using the excuse that his parents needed him around the home because his mother was sick. Out of all the trials of that time, it was this quiet lie that left him feeling so guilty. His mother was his guiding light, and he had been brought up in a home that was fearful of tempting fate with untruths, a throwback to his grandmother's standing in their village. But it was his sensitivity to not hurting Emma's feelings that played heavy on his mind and made him engage in behaviours that were outside of his upbringing.

No matter how good his methods of evasion, fate perhaps got even when Emma had cornered him at his graduation party; she was drunk and flirtatious and had managed to sidewind him in the college car park as he was leaving.

Through slurred speech, she tried to tell him how much she loved him, that she wanted him to *have* her, and began to unbutton her blouse. He fended her off saying that he wasn't interested, but he thanked her for her openness and that he hoped she found someone who would make her happy, but it could not be him.

Then, things got ugly and Emma's true nature came to the fore like an uncaged animal. She ripped open her blouse, the buttons smattering against Bart's chest and she began screaming at him, demanding to know what was wrong with her, what was wrong with *him*, why couldn't they just have sex and be done with it all.

Bart turned tail and ran, fear driving him onwards. In the time he ran the mile back to his home, he'd convinced himself that he was going to be arrested for sexual assault, bringing shame to his family, his academic future ruined.

In panic, when he got home, he grabbed his belongings, leaving behind a note for his parents that he was a good son and not to judge him too harshly. And then he left the family home and headed to Sheffield where he crashed at the parent's house of a male friend he knew from college.

He nurtured anxiety for quite some time, and it would be several weeks before he plucked up the courage to call his mother to tell her he was okay. Her demeanour had been cool to begin with but she warmed in the realisation her boy was alive and well. She made no comment about Emma or the reason he had left home, she only wanted to know he was okay and when he was coming back.

It was this question that had him reticent; his life in a new city was his first taste of freedom, from college and from his family, and he was enjoying it. He told his mother that he would come home, he would certainly stay in touch, but he wanted to see the world for a while before continuing his studies. His primary passion was always geoscience and he passed English, mathematics, and chemistry as straight A's. His plan was to spend a few years saving what he could to fund a geology degree at the University of Plymouth.

After a year waiting tables in Sheffield, he was offered a job at the same coffee shop chain in London. The draw of the capital was immediate, and he moved after serving his notice. Keeping his parents up to date as promised. By this time, it was clear that whatever had happened to Emma Brogan that night on the college car park, she'd calmed down and not taken her flight of fancy any further. Yet its implications remained, the event making him cautious around the many women he met during his job serving tables.

Again, fate had other plans for him the day a man in his fifties came into the London café and ordered an espresso and a slice of lemon drizzle cake. As Bart had carried the drink and food to the table, he saw that there was a book laid out and the images showed a deep trench with men and women clutching excavation tools.

Bart placed the espresso and down, the man adjusting the book slightly to accommodate the small cup and the plate of cake that followed.

"Open trench mining," Bart said, nodding to the image. "Rubies?"

A broad grin brought the man's face alive. "Indeed it is, young man. Now, are you able to tell me where?"

"Burma, or is it Myanmar these days? That's where the best rubies can be found, or so I hear."

"So, it seems you are geographer who waits tables," the man said.

"Well, you're warm but not hot," Bart said. The game broke up the monotony of his afternoon. "If I was to say rubies are, in fact, the mineral *corundum* or *aluminium oxide*, would you change your guess?"

"A geologist?" the man said, exasperated. "Well this is a first, I have to say."

Bart held up a hand. "I'm not a geologist yet, sir. I'm saving to do my degree."

A sense of calm came over the man. When he spoke, the delivery was that of a businessman.

"I have a better idea. Let us meet after you finish up here, and we can discuss what you want to do with your academic studies. How does that sound?"

Bart found it difficult to contain his curiosity. "That would be wonderful, Mr -?"

"Professor Marcus Appleby, but please call me Marcus."

"Then I finish up here in two hours, Marcus. Where shall we meet?"

"Oh, no, my good man," Appleby said. "Take off that apron and walk out of this establishment this instant. As of this minute, if you agree of course, you work for me."

"Why would you do that, sir?"

Appleby smiled and it was warm and sincere. "I've be around a long time. And I can tell when someone is destined to do great things with their life. It makes sense that I give people opportunity to channel this potential so that my company benefits, yes?"

Without question, Bart had undone his apron and allowed it to slip to the floor. Every molecule, every atom in his being was telling him it was the right thing to do. This was further reinforced after his discussion with Appleby later that same day, over dinner at The Ritz, where the professor had a contract drawn up, outlining his apprenticeship in Appleby Enterprises. And the salary once the apprenticeship was over.

Looking back, Bart realised most of the issues leading up to the day his life changed came down to his upbringing. He'd never truly blamed Emma for his fate. Yes, in those early days, when he was frightened and confused, but it was diffused as his experience of the world became bigger, bringing him to places new.

In many ways, he thanked her for putting him on this path that would eventually prove to give him so much by way of opportunity. He would never have met Professor Appleby and the great influence he was to have over Bart's life. Their combined passion for geology would see the professor engineer Bart's geological career, helped by financing degrees in institutions where Appleby had a patronage.

That was not to say Bart did not work hard, his academic achievements were his own, a First-class honours degree in Geology his initial reward, followed by an MSc. and PhD over the next four years. His career had flourished and, as he passed through the hectic lifestyle of work and wealth, he only found others who were completely loyal to the man who had given a chance to an inquisitive waiter in a London café.

He kept his promise and visited home when he could. His mother and father had been earnestly following his academic achievements and subsequent career successes and were always brimming with pride. Their son had become an erudite man of science, a beacon of hope to those who had fled from tyranny and oppression. And Bart also made sure his parents no longer had to work if they didn't want to, paying off their mortgage and sending money home to maintain their well-being. He was the good son, the loyal son.

Such loyalty had brought Bart to the mountain. Appleby was here somewhere, and he would not leave without the man who had given him, and his parents, everything. He was sure that all team members felt this way. Though, in truth, he wasn't too sure about their pilot. Collins was difficult to read behind the wall of cynicism he tended to erect during conversations.

Collins finished up his cigarette. "So, how long are we going to give them?" He flicked his butt-end across the snow. "This bird can't spend too long on the mountain. She's good but not *that* good."

Bart kept his eyes on the rugged slopes. "We take our lead from Havers, I guess. He says we leave, then we leave."

Collins jabbed a thumb at the fuselage behind him. "Havers might oversee *you* but he's not in charge of this bird. If they outstay their welcome or the weather turns to shit, I'm out of here. With or without you. Nothing personal, I have to protect my business interests."

Bart laughed heartily, head thrown back, his chest pumping with mirth. When he got his breath back his gaze met the chopper pilot.

"Professor Appleby has a loyal workforce, Mr Collins."

Collins' face wasn't catching up with the humour. "Yeah? Well, I ain't one of 'em. I'm sub-contracted to fly out here and save all your asses. That means I'm self-employed. This bird is mine and when it comes to her, I'm boss. And that's non-negotiable, man. We clear?"

"As clear as the big sky, Mr Collins."

Collins looked at the smile on his companion's lips and turned in a huff.

"Weird fucker," he muttered under his breath, but the silence allowed it to carry further than he'd intended. The smile on Bart's face broadened when the insult came to him across the snowscape.

Such pettiness was unbecoming of the great mountain above them. The whole area commanded respect, the massif was a geoscientist's dream. The Himalayas stretched for over 2400 kilometres and were a prime example of plate tectonic theory. Geologists held that the continental crust met two tectonic plates, creating the mountain range, while weather and erosion did the rest.

For Bart, the magnificence of the region, over a period of seventy-million years, showed the true significance of man in the grand scheme. Compared to Machapuchare, humanity was a child standing in the shadow of its omnipotent parent, small and dependent.

There was unexpected movement, betrayed by the hiss of sliding snow and the smattering of small rocks hitting the exposed magma. Bart observed that Collins was also aware, the pilot was in the process of pulling his handgun from its shoulder-holster.

"What the hell was that?" Collins yelled.

"It's a snow slide, Mr Collins. A quirk of nature. And something you definitely cannot stop with a bullet."

But Bart knew that something had to have caused the disturbance. They watched as a mist of ice rose several hundred yards out, turning the hem of the rockface to a haze. Fear nudged his heart; there was already clear evidence of a recent avalanche, and he hoped that this was nothing more than the landscape making some adjustments before it decided to accept its new form.

The eruption of flame and steam a few feet away from him told a different story. The scientist in him made immediate, geological calculations, digging deep to establish the mountain's volcanic history and he came up blank. Another explosion cut short his analysis as self-preservation had him jumping to his right.

Shapes were emerging from the snowscape. At first Bart thought it was the white, dusty snow swirling about them that made their outline appear indistinct. But when he saw the fur and the way the advancing figures ploughed through the snow drifts, his mind came to some hard conclusions almost immediately.

"Incredible," he whispered.

A salvo of bright beams cut through the air, three punched into the chopper, gouging metal and sending spectacular blooms of sparks in all directions, much to the dismay of Collins.

"You think bullets can stop *that*, smartass?" Collins hollered at him.

Bart doubted it but he drew his own gun anyway, a SIG Sauer P365, a token thing to reflect his capability. He was, after all, a geologist.

Another arc-blast, another detonation against the fuselage of Collins' helicopter. "For fuck's sake. Leave my bird alone, will ya?"

Collins took aim and fired three times, controlled, and measured in his response despite his anger. Bart watched as one of the creatures stumbled but continued. The beings were becoming clearer now - shaggy beasts but they carried weapons of shimmering blue metal. It was from these weapons that the arc-blasts flew at alarming speed, reminding Bart of laser fire from so many space movies. The whole image was out of whack, only his fear of what these things were planning to do to him and Collins taking the edge off his sense of amazement.

"Reloading!" Collins called out. "You going to use that gun for anything other than keeping your hand occupied until you get back to your room, asshole?"

Bart kicked up a gear. He took aim, and let go two rounds, both of which went wide. He tried to concentrate, another burst of arc-fire crackling over his head. He fired again, three shots this time, and one of them tore fur from the thigh of one of the creatures. It continued to advance as though unaware it had been hit.

More small arms fire now as Collins re-joined the fray, the sounds pitiful against the searing blasts of heat zipping across the massif. Small tears appeared on the chests of the relentless duo, but they showed no signs of stopping, striding through the snow like bathers wading through surf, their great steps carving troughs in the pristine surface.

"To hell with this," Collins said. "Cover me, will ya? And by that, I mean try and fucking hit something while I'm gone."

The pilot didn't wait, he yanked open the rear door and clambered inside. Bart continued to return fire and, as before, it proved to be ineffective. The creatures were now only a few hundred yards out and showing no sign of fear.

Collins was suddenly beside him. In his hands he cradled a rifle, a bulky thing gleaming with gun-grease. Collins primed it, went down to one knee, and opened up with several short bursts. The creatures appeared to hesitate, the surface of their bodies rippling as the bullets found their target.

"Ha! I thought this might even things up a little," Collins chimed. "How'd you like the AR-15, fellas? It's brought a friend along too!"

With that, a puff of smoke came from the underside of the rifle, followed by a popping sound. Seconds later, a bloom of flame appeared on the midriff of the creature on the left; the explosion that followed was dull, and the slewed torso toppled to the ground.

Green liquor pumped from the creature's ruined stomach and, to the amazement of both men, something appeared to slither out onto the ice, a thing with long limbs, shrouded in yellow steam. Collins broke its body apart with another burst of fire.

"There's something inside those things," Bart said in awe. "Something's controlling them?"

His colleague primed another grenade into the launcher. "At this point, I seriously don't give one. We can do the field trip once we take this other fucker out."

Another arc-blast slammed into the chopper; this time the machine lost its tail fin and, before Collins could voice his rage, a tremendous explosion lifted both men into the air and shoved them backwards in a cloud of burning debris.

Bart landed, the soft snow taking the brunt of the impact, but then it yielded, and he found his body jarred by solid rock, knocking the wind out of him. Groaning, he tried to sit up and get his bearings, but as soon as he moved, the ground gave out with a long, grinding moan.

The next moment, the solid surface beneath him was gone and he was in freefall, the light above diminishing as he quickly fell into darkness.

***

Chris listened out as a series of sharp pops and a low rumble came in from the direction of their landing zone.

"What was that?"

Elspeth followed the sound, her eyes making a note of the slate sky overhead. "Thunder?"

Dan shook his head. "That wasn't thunder. That was small arms fire and an explosion."

"Look!" Elspeth pointed to a smear of smoke as it drifted from behind the rocky outcrop.

"The chopper," Chris said flatly. "Come on, we need to get back down there."

But, without a word, Dan continued *up* the slope.

"Hey, Dan!" Chris called. "Lake! Hold up!"

Dan made no attempt to stop his advance to higher ground.

"For Christ's sake," Chris said through clenched teeth. He followed Dan. By the time he caught up with him, Chris was out of breath.

"When was the last time you hauled ass, Commander?" He went to walk off.

"Will you wait a minute?" Chris' voice was firm enough for Dan to pause.

"While we wait, our employers could be in the shit," Dan said.

"Think I don't know that?"

"Then act like you do."

The pause was longer than it seemed. But when Chris spoke, he had reined in his irritation.

"We have to take stock. Make decisions based on operational parameters. Christ, you know this already, why am I having this discussion with you, damn it?"

"I've a duty to the Applebys and so do you."

"You need to stabilise your thinking, Dan," Chris said resolutely. "We need *everybody* in order to achieve on this mountain."

Dan took a breath and his response was measured though infused with suppressed anger.

"The chopper's gone. Chances are Bart and Collins are gone, too. You know it. The only way off this rock is by following the asset tracker."

"Well I'm not prepared to leave anyone behind unless I'm sure, Dan. That's not how I do things."

"Then you'll be getting yourself killed too, and for nothing. I guess you do what you gotta do, Chris. Just like I intend."

Chris watched Dan stomp off. "Christ, what a mess."

"What you going to do?" Elspeth said cautiously from behind him.

"I'll go and see what's happening with the chopper. Can you handle Dan?"

"Can you?" She smiled.

Chris wagged a finger at her. "Touché."

He turned, his intention to head back the way they had come.

"Chris."

He paused. "Yeah?"

Her voice was sullen, yet sincere. "Be careful."

He acknowledged her with a mock salute. Within moments he was heading back down the plateau.

CHAPTER FIVE

They entered the chamber, Knowles with the arc-rifle primed and ready, the high roof lost to sight. Veins of silver streaked through the walls, giving off a watery light, but Knowles knew this to be the result of alien influence on the mountain. She took its presence for what it was, a beacon to help them navigate their way through this eerie netherworld.

Deeper into the cave, Knowles could see that the central space was not completely unoccupied. There were shapes scattered around, hewn from rocks, stalagmites rose here and there like the fauna of some alien forest. These thick cylinders had been fashioned into seats or tables, central meeting areas for the village, and Knowles realised this could have been a human equivalent of a town square or subterranean arboretum.

It shouldn't have surprised her that the Yeti would be a communal species, she'd seen evidence of that from Sully. Still, she was coming to terms with a lot of things these days. The existence of creatures of folklore and invading extra-terrestrials were just a few of the adjustments she was having to make on a minute-by-minute basis.

Then there was the real reason they were here, deep in the earth. Retribution, the loss of her true family, Grant Hastings and Patrick Vine, brothers in arms and kindred, snatched from the world for doing nothing more than trying to enact the right thing, to help someone in distress.

She recalled her words to Hastings as he lay dying in her arms. *"We need to get you out of here. Fuck knows how, but we've got to try. That's what The Sebs do, right?"*

But her friend was no longer able to comprehend, his last breath telling her to save herself. That was what they did for each other. Family first, always.

"You hurt?"

Sully's voice startled her, giving her response a caustic edge. "What?" She softened as she understood what he meant. "No, I'm not sad, just thinking. Just coming to terms with things."

She wasn't sure if he understood the words or the context, but she said them regardless, and she supposed that, in the end, she'd really said them for herself. A kind of mourning for a world that was, a world of ghosts.

Yet, as she looked upon him, his great stature diminished by the sudden slump in his shoulders, Knowles realised that Sully, too, was in the same emotional space. This village was a reminder of the way things used to be for him and his kind before the alien invaders had decimated their race.

She felt both saddened and selfish in that moment; her friend was hurting, and she had been preoccupied by her own sense of loss. This was what would become of humanity should these alien bastards get their way, reduced to abandoned homes and community spaces turned to dust.

Through her ruminations, an archway caught her attention. It was different to the others in that at its apex was a strange symbol. She headed over to it and saw that the image had been carved into a flat, rectangular plinth buffed into the rock, and consisted of a straight, horizontal line with three more rising from it. The lines at either end were set at thirty degrees, the one in the centre was vertical.

"What's that?" Knowles said, pointing out the symbol.

Sully peered up at the motif. "Elder."

"So, this is where the village boss lived?" Knowles said softly. "Shall we go inside?"

She stepped forward but sensed hesitancy in her companion. "What?"

"Disrespectful to go in home of the Elder without invitation."

Knowles thought this through before gently responding. "Well, he isn't here, Sully."

"She. Elder is female."

"The boss is a girl, eh? I'm liking your race already," Knowles chuckled. "Look, Sully, it'll be okay. Promise I'll not touch anything we find. You have my word."

He nodded but there was still reticence in his eyes. Knowles pretended she'd not seen it and walked up to the threshold, peering inside to make sure things were safe.

The first thing she noticed was that the light did not diminish as she stepped into the dwelling. In the enclosed space, the veins of silver running through the walls seemed to concentrate the illuminance, the way a cupped palm will collect water. Because of this, Knowles was able to clearly see the structure within the archway, a broad oval, stretching back for a good ten feet; the walls and floor smoothed out as though someone had hotwired a sand grinder and gone to town on the infrastructure.

Roughly carved tables and chairs, twice the size of even the largest human being, were placed about the living area, where shelving had been secured to the walls with large metal spikes. Everything had an oversized appearance.

"Now I know how Goldilocks felt," Knowles mused to herself; her fingertips traced the rough leg of a dining table which, with its wooden bowls and tankards, appeared still set for a meal that never came.

On the left ellipse there were drapes made from pelts. Knowles went to them and drew the heavy furs back on their misshapen hangers, stepping back as a shower of dust fell from overhead.

Waving away the cloud of rock dust, she peeked inside and found a bedroom which came with a sour, heavy odour that wrinkled her nose. The bed was nothing more than a pile of furs of varying sorts, some white, some grey but most were brown, and even Knowles knew that Sully's kin would not use the fur of their own kind in such a manner.

Knowles gave Sully a wink. "Bedroom, eh? I guess this is where our Elder saw all the action."

The puzzled expression was back on his huge face. "Elder special, wise. She commands. No fighting, too old."

"That makes sense," Knowles said. "Seems strange."

"What strange?"

"This place is tidy. Clean. No sign of struggle."

"Not understand."

She cautiously placed a finger on one of the furs. "It's like they just got up one day and just left. Calm as you'd like. No fighting."

This made no sense. Sully had proven that yetis were powerful, and even with the advent of those cod-eyed invaders, it seemed unlikely they would merely give up their homes without resistance of some kind.

Given that Sully had no answer for her either meant, to her at least, this kind of conciliatory behaviour was out of character for these fantastic creatures. Something must have happened, something more than the threat of alien invasion.

Movement beyond the mountain of furs interrupted her thoughts, a disturbance on the surface of the far wall. It was slight, no more than a smattering of debris, a thin cataract of dirt falling to the ground with a series of clicks as grit peppered the rocks. Rather than step away, Knowles edged forward, arc-rifle aimed at a spot six feet from the ground where an aperture was forming in the dolomite.

Without warning, the thin stream of grit became a torrent, larger pieces of rock now tumbling onto the rock and furs. This time Knowles did jump back and not a moment too soon.

A section of the entire wall fell in, a great, uneven slab of rock smashing into the bedroom, leaving a gaping hole behind it. There was no watery light coming through the newly formed fissure, just an eternal blackness, a ghastly toothless mouth that seemed frozen in an eternal, soundless scream.

The breeze that emanated from the opening was fetid, making Knowles and Sully gag, a terrible mix of sulphur and sweat, grabbing them, almost making them dizzy with its foulness.

Then there was movement from within the endless dark, accompanied by a scuttling sound, as though many tiny bones were hitting a harsh surface. Something was emerging from the blackness, something with great size and bulk. As the beast was given form by the milky light from the bedroom walls, Knowles looked on in horror.

There were legs, she counted eight, and they were thick with multiple joints. It was an arachnid of sorts, a high spherical abdomen, striped like a zebra, the silvery light giving it a terrible beauty. But there was no cephalothorax, instead there was a furred torso, complete with arms, and the face of a yeti, face a black smudge, but the eyes bright and fierce, the jaws rammed with savage, yellowed fangs.

Before she could make sense of what was happening, the thing attacked. And it proved to be as fast as it was deadly.

***

Pilot Steve Collins had always loved aircraft. His passion was an enigma to his family who, in contrast, preferred to remain grounded in the realms of reality. His father worked as a long-distance lorry driver for a major supermarket chain; his mother ran two jobs, one as a school dinner lady, and at night she was signed up to an agency providing cleaners for local businesses.

Collins was one of three children. Robert, his younger brother, was killed in a road traffic collision when he had just left college. He'd been found to be three times over the drink-drive limit. No other vehicle was involved in the crash. Alison, his older sister, pretty much brought up her younger brothers given their parents were out most of the time bringing home the bacon.

Despite this, his upbringing was stable, his parents being able to put money aside for family trips to the British coast every summer, and there were modest gifts at Christmas, albeit deferred payment options via a Littlewoods catalogue.

Whatever allowances were available to him Collins spent on items related to aircraft. Books, models (*Airfix* and *Revell* kits were his favourite) and watching TV shows such as *Airwolf* and low-quality reruns of *The Whirly Birds*.

It was perhaps the exhilaration of watching the air-sea rescue reality show *Rescue*, where the daredevil responses of RAF Sea King helicopter pilots were at the forefront, that made him want to become a chopper pilot. For a kid from a working-class background this seemed as far-fetched as trying to become an astronaut without a mathematics major. As it turned out, it was an incredible case of bad luck that ironically made his dream a reality.

The event that made it all happen was the death of his father when Collins was sixteen years of age. Mr Collins Senior's eighteen-wheeler had careened off the southbound carriageway of the M42 just outside the market town of Bromsgrove, mounting the central reservation and putting it on the northbound carriageway where it rolled. Ten people were killed, thirty were injured. The accident investigators found nothing to suggest driver error, though it did take several weeks to draw such a conclusion. What they did find, however, was that the rear axle of the trailer had sheared due to ill maintenance. The subsequent investigation by the Health and Safety Executive did the rest to support a compensation claim.

The case was settled out of court for an undisclosed sum. In truth, the Collins family received a two million pound pay off. For a family used to working endless hours to provide the basics, this was a bittersweet windfall. The money cushioned the blow as their grief struck home.

His mother placed one-hundred thousand in a Trust fund for each of her kids to access on their eighteenth birthday. On the morning that Collins was able to retrieve the funds, he used a chunk to enrol in flight school and in two years gained his commercial pilot's licence. He flew with a budget airline for three years, and in his downtime learned to fly choppers out of a private helicopter school in Chelmsford. Within five years, he was working for an oil company, contracted to fly to rigs out in the North Sea. This was where the challenges really began; adverse weather conditions and the excitement of flying over open water was the very thing he'd always wanted when he was a kid. The money wasn't bad either.

He used the time to gain his instructor qualifications and build up a small flying school, his intention to use this as a retirement venture. Then he saw the freelance opportunities elsewhere in the world. Always restless, always seeking adventure, he found himself in a variety of jobs, most legal, others not quite so much.

He knew how to fly, was exceptional at it (gifted some would say) but on occasions, especially carrying spurious cargo over Colombia for example, the need to learn other skills, those to increase the success of self-preservation in particular, came to the fore. And there were people to teach him; how to shoot, how to fight, how to stay the fuck alive.

By the time he'd taken on work for Appleby Enterprises, Collins was an all-round survivor, and loved every second of his work. In the twenty-five years he'd been flying, he'd never lost a bird. Yes, he'd been shot at and nature had almost snatched him from the sky on a few occasions, but he'd always seen it through.

But not today.

Today had seen him not only lose the first aircraft in his entire career, it had been blown to pieces by some fucking monster that shouldn't exist. Now things were going from bad to the biggest pile of shit imaginable.

The explosion had thrown him clear of the chopper, and he'd landed unceremoniously on his front, face planting into powdered snow. Despite the soft landing, he could feel the sting of lacerations to his back and as he reached for a point where his kidneys throbbed, his glove slithered over something wet.

As the explosion faded in his ears, another sound came to him, a rumble that also brought a tremor in the ground beneath him. He watched as the snow about him began to shiver, the white surface oscillating like icing sugar residue on a kitchen worktop as the blender kicked in.

The rumbling became a roar, the whole shelf seemed to move, and he watched the remnants of the Leonardo sink as though in quicksand, the flames snuffed out with an angry sizzle, and then it was gone, swallowed by the unforgiving earth.

But the next moment brought him back to reality as he found the ground beneath him give way with a jolt, making him call out in surprise. The floor held out long enough for him to convince himself it had done its worst, but then he felt himself being sucked into the mountain as the rock gave out.

He fell for what seemed an eternity. The darkness was total, the wind roaring in his ears, whipping away his scream, forcing air into his nasal passages, suffocating him, making him dizzy and disorientated. Something came up to him through the din, a huge explosion of water far below. He thought he could see a dim light, glittering streaks that wavered like shooting stars in the heavens.

A subterranean lake.

Without warning Collins hit something, it was like landing on a mattress; what little air that still remained in his lungs was knocked out of him as he bounced off at an angle, a musty cloud rising with him, his nostrils filled with the odour of old, dank mushrooms. Airborne once more, he could see the lake, and it was giving off its own glow, casting spangled honeycomb patterns onto a nearby rock wall.

The next moment he was submerged in warm water; it embraced him like the comforting arms of a lost lover, his pummelled body welcoming the weightlessness, drifting through a fluid netherworld that possessed his mind as thought drifted away; a man seduced by the notion it may never return.

***

Chris made his way across the snowscape, the rugged precipice rising high to his right, the ground churned up in places from their outward-bound journey. As he walked, he attempted to concentrate on the task ahead, and making sure that the rest of his team, and their ride off the mountain, was safe.

The oily smudge of smoke rising from the landscape didn't bode well. But, if nothing else, Chris knew himself to be a man of optimism. The chopper carried smoke grenades and perhaps Collins had seen fit to detonate one as a means of alerting them. It was a stretch, he knew this, but he compartmentalised it as real leaders should and quickened his pace, attempting to suppress other concerns as he went.

This was, however, proving difficult and the person stirring the pot was, as always, Daniel Lake.

The two men had not worked together for that long, and maybe this was part of the problem. Chris had tried to earn the guy's respect but there was no moving Dan from his steadfast position of never being in the fucking wrong. As he'd already inferred, Chris figured that at the heart of the matter was their previous lives, or rather, their previous *careers* before joining Appleby Enterprises.

A cop and a criminal, a dysfunctional team in anyone's book. On a scarp, at a point of crisis, the fracture in their relationship may as well have been as wide as some of the ravines on this infernal mountain range. He'd hoped that, at some point, Dan might see him as a comrade, he had left the police force and committed to a nefarious employer, after all. Chris had often considered the contradiction in his own decision to work for Appleby given his service to the police.

But the guilt had only ever been fleeting and he was able to rationalise that his individual actions had not broken any laws. His own father had once said that piety was the luxury of the contented. He usually said such things after too much to drink. Which was often enough to have him dying of liver sclerosis fifteen years ago.

"Damn it!" Chris whispered. These ruminations were exactly what he didn't need right now. There were bigger things to consider and there was no going back without some form of resolution, be that either Appleby or his young wife. And dealing with whoever held them. He was fast coming around to the idea Dan had floated, that they were being held against their will.

He was pondering such matters when the hideous din of grinding rock filled the air; the ground beneath jittered beneath his feet and he quickened his pace, despite the danger of falling over. He rounded the plateau and briefly saw the chopper, the main fuselage ablaze, tail fin detached and twisted like a broken finger, and unidentifiable pieces scattered around the area. Then it was gone, pulled beneath the earth as the ground beneath gave way, the snow flowing into the newly opened fissure, disappearing like water as the bath plug is pulled.

But even this scene, with all its incredible, awful implications for their mission, paled in comparison to the lone figure he now saw standing on the crumbling snowfield. It was a figure with white and grey, shaggy fur. At first Chris thought it was a polar bear, then realised that such creatures were alien to this region. Part of him also questioned what it was that this beast was holding in its paws. It looked oddly like some form of spear. No, not a spear but a –

The arc-rifle felled Chris as he was making his assessment. The blast punching through his sternum, shredding bone, and flesh, then searing them back together in one mangled, blackened circle of sizzling meat.

Slinging the arc-rifle on its right shoulder, the war machine powered through the snow until it looked down at the human lying at its feet. The alien inside examined the body for life signs on its internal scanner, noting brain activity in the cranium. Using the controls, the alien stooped, clamping the massive hands either side of the head, and lifted the body from the snow.

It brought the paws together with inhuman force, the resulting crack as loud as a pistol shot.

Discarding the bloody remains, the alien then brought its attention to the tracks leading away from the area. It took a few moments to prioritise its next movements, looking back at the fissure that had swallowed the human flying machine, and then turned to follow the tracks leading off into the mountains.

Gearing up, the war machine continued its march up the slope, the pilot inside as devoid of emotion as the machine it controlled.

CHAPTER SIX

Knowles looked on in horror as the hideous creature extrapolated itself from the gap it had clawed into the Elder's bedroom wall. Everything appeared in super slow-motion, her eyes taking in the awful vision as it became a reality, unfurling and lethal.

The arc-rifle came up, training kicking in, experience doing the rest, but before she could trigger the weapon, the creature scooped up the pelts lying between it and its prey, launching them into the air, cloaking its advance through the chamber.

Jumping back, Knowles let out a cry of surprise as she bounced into the yielding-yet-firm body of Sully who was standing directly behind her. The airborne pelts landed, sending out a massive gust of stale, disgusting air, but the corner of one covering caught Knowle's arm in its descent. She lost grasp of her rifle and it skittered beneath the feet of the great, terrible beast now filling the bed chamber. In dismay, Knowles watched as the arc-rifle was trampled underfoot, a thin crack and high-pitched hiss marking its final passing into ruination.

Sully wrapped his powerful arms about Knowles and stepped back, yanking her out of the bed chamber and into the main living area, his bulky frame bashing into the table, knocking it askew and sending bowls and cups bouncing.

Releasing Knowles, Sully scooped her backwards with a forearm so that he was now standing between her and the oncoming monster. From her viewpoint, Knowles managed to assess the creature as it clambered from the chamber. The simian face was a mask of rage, its maw opening and closing, the cries coming from it were both terrifying and piteous. The eyes were locked into a stare, as though the lids were stapled open, and angry tears flowed like the waters of a bitter spring.

In better light, Knowles could see its body wasn't completely covered in fur; there were extensive bald patches, and through these she observed lesions and open sores that oozed with dark liquid. The thing was as wretched as it was, no doubt, lethal.

Brandishing the club, Sully tried to keep distance as the hybrid stalked them through the dwelling. Knowles felt Sully's left arm herding her towards the doorway leading out into the arboretum. It made sense as only open space would protect them now; trapped inside they were as good as lunch.

But, as Sully edged closer to the exit, the hybrid appeared to sense their intention. It grabbed the table and cast it aside as though it was nothing more than matchwood. The tabletop broke into pieces as it struck the far wall and now there was nothing between them save for a few chairs.

The click of arachnid legs on the floor, the hiss of the simian mouth, these things added a sinister ambience to the event, unsettling Knowles now that she was without a weapon. Her mind worked fast; the chairs might provide something if they were broken up, but it was a reach even for her sense of optimism.

The ultimate decision was made by Sully. Before she knew what was happening, he'd grabbed her collar and shoved her towards the exit. She let out a cry of pain and frustration as she landed outside the dwelling, rolling twice before she stopped, lying on her back, and gazing up at the tooth-like stalactites overhead.

She heard a roar and it galvanised, she sat up and winced at the twinge in her lower back. Despite this, she scrambled to the entrance and looked in as Sully stepped forward, swinging his club into one of the chairs as though on a driving range. The structure lifted from the floor and smashed into the face of the hybrid, blood and teeth flew from its tortured mouth.

During this diversion, Sully launched himself into the fray, club high this time, bringing it down on one of the creature's flailing arms. There was an awful cracking sound and the hybrid emitted a mighty, agonised scream.

"Go get him, slugger!" Knowles shouted, unable to contain her relief that Sully was tipping the balance of things in their favour.

But this was to prove short lived. The creature lashed out with one of its many legs, and the appendage passed through Sully's thigh.

It was Sully's turn to cry out, and instinct had him bringing the club down onto the spider-leg, snapping it in two. He fell away, the lower half of the creature's limb still imbedded in his thigh.

Knowles could see blood pumping down Sully's white fur, and she seethed. But there was also fear. For Sully, for her.

The hybrid may have been maimed but it was far from finished. It now towered over Sully, waiting for the right moment to finish him off. But it was cautious enough to show restraint, learning that Sully was formidable, and the club was still strong in his hands, ready to fight to the end.

Knowles realised that perhaps the hybrid was not being cautious at all, perhaps it was merely waiting for Sully to bleed out, biding its time until it reached the point where he'd become too weak to defend himself, and then pounce.

She was crawling back to the dwelling when she heard something else. A low, ferocious growl that vibrated in her sternum.

And it was coming from behind her.

***

Though he'd never admit it to those around him, Dan was worried. The mission was a shit-show, and outcome measures were beyond poor. He stood on the slope, keeping watch as Elspeth eyed her location device.

It wasn't just their inability to respond to tactical challenges, he'd no doubt that the team currently on the mountain were good at what they did, but they weren't the kind of rescue team that was needed. Dan felt this was more about retrieval rather than rescue and that left him concerned about their commitment to go the extra mile.

Chris didn't help, either. Dan was used to having complete faith in his team leaders. Never had he been in a situation like this, where his only option seemed to be ignoring the person in command based on his own instincts.

Such a situation left him feeling uncomfortable, unsettled. Scared, even. And that was the worst enemy of all at a time of crisis.

"I got something!" Elspeth's thin voice came to him from the incline above. Dan sighed and made his way up the slope where his colleague was tracing a gloved finger across the tablet's screen. She glanced over at Dan, a frown on her face.

He could see the disapproval in her eyes. "Out with it."

"You got yourself an insubordination issue there, Dan. You want to get fired?"

"Just staying focused is all. Things are turning to shit fast out here. Tell me you got some good news?"

She presented the tablet so he could view the screen. "Well, it's not bad news, if that helps?"

He adjusted his position so he could see the images. "It helps plenty."

"Despite occasional drop-out, the asset signal is strong and moving southeast."

"What's the cause of the drop out?"

She withdrew the tablet and tapped her fingers on the readouts. "Atmospherics are good, so satellite bounce should be optimal."

"Which means what?"

"Which means the asset isn't on the surface."

Dan rubbed a hand across his chin. "What? Underground?"

Elspeth nodded. "A cave system, maybe. Something with an entrance that can't be too far away from here."

Dan gave out a dissatisfied grunt. "This whole mission just keeps getting worse."

"I guess we'll need to hold up here, wait for the others."

Dan stomped past her, heading up the slope. "Feel free."

She watched him, exasperated. "Where you going?"

Dan continued up the incline without looking back. "Our boss needs us and I'm not about to sit around here and freeze to death while Havers sticks his thumb up his own arse."

"Last time I looked we were part of a team," she sniped.

He stopped and looked back at her. "Team? Are you sniffing chopper fuel, lady? This is improvisation at best, and it turned sour as soon as we left Pokhara."

Grim-faced, she waved the tablet at him. "So how do you intend to follow the asset without this?"

"I guess I'm going to have to persuade you to give it to me." His face was stone.

She shook her head and secured the pad in her thigh pocket. "Believe me, your negotiation skills currently need significant work."

"Or I could just come down there and take it."

Elspeth laughed, a cold hollow sound of someone who has reached the limit of their patience. "Yeah. Better to drop all this sanctimonious macho bullshit and radio Chris. See what the hell is going on. Take it from there?"

Dan chewed his lip. She was right, of course. He couldn't do this alone and she knew it.

"So, are you going to call it in?" she pressed.

"Okay, damn it." Dan pulled his radio from his breast pocket and spoke into it, his words clipped. "Havers, this is Lake. Come in. Over."

A sharp burst of static was the only response. He tried again. "Havers. I need a SITREP. Come in, over."

The fizz in the handset changed for a few seconds. As both waited for Chris' voice to air, a sustained high-pitched squeal came from the radio and Dan threw it away from him. The plastic ignited and by the time it landed on the rocks, it was a ball of incandescent flame.

"What happened?" Elspeth said, aghast.

"Device malfunction?" he offered.

"Hell, if you're going to guess, at least make it plausible." Elspeth's mouth opened, but she was looking behind him, her jaw dropping as though she'd palsied. "What the hell is *that*?"

Dan followed her gaze. Then saw the bloodied creature walking across the plateau, walking towards them, a smear of gore in its wake.

Elspeth produced a sidearm. She looked at the creature stomping towards them, then back down at the Glock 19.

"I think we're in trouble," she whispered.

Dan took aim with his assault rifle and opened fire on the approaching menace. The torso bubbled with multiple strikes, but the creature's pace didn't abate.

"We're definitely in trouble," Elspeth concluded.

Dan called out to her. "Come on, let's get to higher ground."

She stooped and began navigating the icy rocks, hoping to put obstacles between her and the beast. Dan was alongside, having quickly decided to conserve ammunition and opting for a tactical retreat.

The arc-rifle spat plasma over their heads, and Elspeth shouted out with surprise as rocks ahead of them shattered.

They were having to climb, the slope giving way to a significant incline of black rock, frosted with ice. Dan looked up. Overhead was a shelf of snow. Below was the creature, coming for them, an unstoppable, savage entity, determined to bring about their destruction.

The crackle of an arc-rifle, another bright blast of plasma, threatening to douse them both in scalding steam as snow and ice vaporised about them.

Elspeth almost let out another cry of despair when she rounded a rocky outcrop and saw two more creatures lying in the snow. Her mind was convinced they were part of an ambush but then she saw that both mounds of fur were charred and smeared with green liquid.

"They're everywhere," she said as Dan joined her.

He ducked behind a rock and watched as the creature came up the ravine; it was now grabbing the rugged surface with one great paw, bracing off with its legs as it dragged itself along, rifle held in one hand and aimed at the summit.

Dan sighted the snow shelf and unloaded several shots from the rifle. Bullets smattered the snow and for a moment it looked as though the assault had achieved nothing. As the creature came within forty feet or so, teeth bared and the rifle ready to deliver another deadly salvo, there was a great cracking noise and the whole shelf slid off the outcrop, dumping tons of snow into the ravine, covering the creature as though it were a bad dream. Clouds of ice came up to them, Dan and Elspeth having to fall back from its frosty haze.

Gasping, they stood, bodies bowed and minds still trying to come to terms with the incredible sight they had just witnessed.

"What was that?" she asked incredulously.

"You know what it was, you saw it," Dan whispered.

She nodded towards the other fallen carcasses. "Things are not what they seem here."

"It changes nothing. We have to stay on track."

Elspeth went over to the other creatures, her gun trained on the exposed abdomens.

"There's something inside. This isn't organic, it's a machine."

"And what the fuck is that?" Dan said, nudging the alien with his foot.

"The pilot. We're out of our depth here. We can't go on without backup."

"Back up? From where?" Dan said. "You saw the blood on the thing that came for us. We've got to accept we've lost everyone on the slopes. The chopper has gone. Our only hope of staying alive is to get under this mountain."

"These things might have Appleby," Elspeth cautioned.

"Or they were killed by the people who do. Someone nailed these bastards, and not so long ago by the looks of it, so I'm hopeful." Dan's response had the weight of confidence behind it, but Elspeth was still uncertain.

"I not so sure -" she began but was interrupted as shuffling sounds came from the ravine and, to their disbelief, a mighty paw punched through the snow as the creature who had pursued them fought to be free of its icy prison.

"Determined little fucker, isn't it?" Dan said.

Elspeth stepped backwards and spotted the pool of yellow fluid. "I found something back here."

Without taking his eyes away from their assailant, Dan scuttled up beside her.

He glanced down at the pool. "Any ideas?"

"A way into the mountain?" she suggested.

Dan looked back at the limbs now flailing in the snow thirty feet away from them. The creature broke free, arc-rifle still clutched in one paw, and then they were truly out of options.

"But we can't be sure," he said.

Elspeth pointed. "Look at the ground."

Dan did as Elspeth asked and noted the snow about the pool was churned. In places there were boot prints that were not theirs.

Dan seemed relieved. "Well at least we know there were people here."

"And they went through."

Assured, Dan faced the pool. "Then I guess we do the same."

Elspeth gave him a wan smile. "If I'm going to die, I'd prefer to do it in the warm."

With that, she stepped into the pool. Dan followed moments later.

* * *

Collins felt his life slipping away. With this release came an overwhelming sense of peace, of relief if truth be told, and acceptance rose to embrace its legitimacy.

From nowhere, tranquillity was suddenly shattered. Collins felt harsh, clutching fingers manhandling him, yanking him upwards. Suddenly his face broke free of the water, the coolness of the breeze bringing him to his senses.

"What the fuck's going on?" He heard his voice, but it sounded far away, as though coming from the world of never-ending peace, the realm of death.

The tone in his ear was calming, familiar. "Just work with me, Steve. Don't fight it."

Collins allowed himself to be pulled through the water, the splashes echoing about them.

Then he was free of the lake and being dragged across harsh ground, his lower back protesting at the journey. He moaned with pain as he was propped up against rock.

"Sorry." The soft voice again. "Just had to get you out of there. I thought you were dead."

"No, I *was* dead. Now I just feel like shit," he muttered.

"You're welcome." Bart chuckled.

Collins' eyes blinked away water. "Where's all the light coming from?"

"These silver veins in the rocks. Warm to touch. Like they're alive."

"That's not a good image."

Bart looked around him, awe-struck. "Never thought the mountain held such secrets. The geology here is a scientific goldmine."

Collins rubbed at his face. "It's a fucking pit, Bart. And we're stuck at the bottom of it."

Undeterred, Bart looked about the cavern. "There will be a way out. This lake will feed into springs, there will be a tunnel network. We just have to follow it."

Bart stood, and wandered to the water's edge. Collins noticed that the big man was limping.

"You didn't get through it unscathed, either, eh?"

Stooping, Bart cupped a hand and dipped it into the lake. "No. Just a sprain. But we really should be dead." He looked up where a tiny slash of white light streaked across the dark ceiling.

"That fall was a good hundred metres. Hitting the water would be like hitting concrete." He tipped the water from his hand and massaged his fingers together.

"What is it?" Collins said.

"There's a viscosity to this water."

"In English?" The pain in his lower back was making Collins more irritable than usual.

"It has different properties to normal water," Bart explained. "It's more like cerebrospinal fluid. The shock absorber for your spine."

"And?"

"I'd suggest that this water had been changed at an atomic level."

Collins clenched his teeth in frustration. "For fuck's sake, Bart. Meaning what?"

"Nature didn't do this. Science did." There was no hiding the amazement in his voice.

"What kind of science?"

"My guess is the kind that blew up our helicopter."

"*My* helicopter," Collins grumbled. He shuffled in his makeshift seat, wincing at the ache in his back. The air about his clothing was musty. "Think I hit some fucking giant mushrooms on the way down. As if things weren't *Jules Verne* enough."

Bart hobbled over to him. "Let me take a look at your back, see what the damage is."

Flinching in panic, Collins held up a hand. "What? Are you a doctor now?"

"Well I have a PhD, so I'm technically already a doctor."

"You know what I mean, smart ass."

Bart grinned. "I know first aid, just like you. Basic stuff. Want me to help you or not?"

Collins answered by lifting the hem of his flight jacket and turning onto his side. Throughout the manoeuvre his teeth were gritted together, but a small stuttering sigh came from the back of his throat.

Bart probed Collins' right flank. As well as many smaller lacerations about his shoulders and back, a gory slash had torn through his shirt. Pulling the material free of the fatigues, Bart examined the wound.

He gently pressed the wound site. "Seems like a clean slice."

Collins moved away from the probing fingers as though branded. "Fuck me, what the hell are you doing, man?"

"Checking the depth of the cut and if there's any shrapnel."

"Why don't you just drag me back to the fucking lake and drown me?" Collins chided.

Bart sat back on his haunches. "As tempting as it may be at this point, it's not in my nature to be unnecessarily violent. Now, are you going to let me help you?"

Collins sighed again. This time it was with resignation. "Okay, let's get it over with. What you going to do?"

"The wound isn't deep and it's clear of shrapnel. I guess I'll clean it and stitch it up."

"You've done that before?" Collins said with some reservation.

"I've stitched many things. My mother taught me."

"You're talking about socks and shit, aren't you?"

"It's the same principle, have a little faith." Bart fished around in his pockets and pulled out a small leather pack. Inside was a sewing kit.

"You keep a needle and thread with you?" said Collins.

"You never know when you might get a hole in your sock." Bart winked.

Collins shook his head, dumbfounded.

Bart paused as he began opening the kit and retrieving a needle and bobbin. "Right. I'm not going to lie to you, this is going to be a little uncomfortable."

"You mean it's going to hurt like fuck?" Collins said quietly.

"That too," Bart said, threading the needle.

CHAPTER SEVEN

Clutching his bloodied leg, Sully shuffled backwards, the hybrid stalking him through the yeti dwelling, one arm hanging limp, its eyes simmering with hate.

Part of Sully was aware of Knowles as she yelled out in surprise from the arboretum. His instinct was to clamber to his feet and get to her, protect her from whatever new foe had come to do battle with them.

His thoughts were deep, a far cry from what humans would consider hidden inside his incredible physique. To people, Sully was just a vicious animal, no different to the hybrid now moving towards him, intent only on doling out slaughter.

To the creatures who fell from the sky, those who wiped out his kin over centuries, wearing their skin and turning them into macabre machines of war, Sully's kind were nothing more than slaves, subservient creatures to be browbeaten and butchered in the name of science or warfare.

Sully heard Knowles cry out again, and he clutched at his club, trying to turn weapon into crutch to help him stand. He growled in pain as his leg turned to fiery agony as he executed the manoeuvre. He could not risk taking his eyes off the hybrid.

The creature gave out a huge roar, skittering through the dwelling, its fear of Sully now waning as it saw its fallen adversary weakly brace off the club to support its weight. It went for the kill, full-pelt and without warning.

With his balance compromised, Sully was taken off his feet, the impact of the charge smashing him into the wall to the left of the exit. A cloud of dust fell from the ceiling, a shroud for his pending demise. Groggy, and disorientated, Sully felt himself being lifted, powerful, leathery hands grabbing cruelly at his fur, pulling at him, making him cry out in rage. He brought up a mighty fist, only to have it swiped away, and through it all came loud guttural shouts.

For the first time in many years, the mighty Sully felt helpless.

***

"Can you believe this place?" Elspeth reached out and placed her hand against the seam where rock and metal fused together.

Dan stepped from the landing disc. "After fighting off gun-toting yeti robots, I can believe just about anything."

Their transition through the pool had been as uneventful as walking down a flight of stairs. The technology may have fascinated but it was a means to an end. And there was no escaping the fact that, at that moment, no end appeared to be in sight.

The space about them was modest, a room that appeared to have no other function than to serve the circular transportation grill set into the plinth. There was a corridor leading off the room and neither of them could see the end of it, just one long stretch into apparent infinity.

Elspeth consulted her tablet. The asset tracker was blinking steadily, indicating a locality. She noted something else.

"The asset is stationary."

"What?"

"You heard me. The abductee has stopped moving." She tapped her screen just to be sure.

Dan was pensive for a moment. "Could be taking a break. They've been hauling arse for over four hours."

"Or it could mean the asset is injured. Or worse."

Dan rounded on her. "What is it with you people? You're so damn keen to write all of this off."

Elspeth stood before him, face stern. "I won't speak for anyone else, Dan. But I call things as I see them. I'm neither a pessimist nor an optimist, I'm a realist led by the data."

"Like a robot. You're no better than those things above ground," Dan spat.

"Didn't see you shed any tears for the people we lost up there," she said coolly.

"I didn't *know* any of them. But what I *do* know is they were inexperienced and a liability. They paid for that."

Elspeth took a breath before responding, matter of fact. "Let's not go throwing accusations of sociopathy around, or you're just going to add 'hypocrite' to your long list of shitty attributes."

"Fuck you, Elspeth."

Her face in neutral, Elspeth double checked her tablet. "Two miles, northeast. You coming?"

She moved out without looking back, her strides long, her shoulders back. A statement of strength and independence. A dismissal of everything Dan stood for, every belief that he held.

Elspeth had grown up in a strong family ethic. She never understood the concept of individualism on an operation, and that Dan would behave in such a way left her angry. But it also left her wary of the man, of how he would react when they found their asset, and the actuality if such a discovery didn't match his beliefs.

The odds were ratcheting on this being nothing but a poor outcome. Dan was right in that, as missions went, this was already far from a success. In fact, it bordered on catastrophe and Elspeth had felt duty bound to point this out.

Dan's response had surprised her, but she was way beyond taking offense at such things, no one could despise her as much as she despised herself, after all. But one of the positives for keeping the mission on track was it highlighted that her companion did have it in him to care for the Applebys, so it meant he could feel something for others. Even if these were the people who paid his wages.

Dan broke into her thoughts. "Looks like there's something up ahead." His voice was measured, without residue from their previous exchange. A truce, it seemed.

Sure enough, the corridor was broadening, each wall fanning out to create a rhombus. Against each wall was a workstation, complete with computer terminal and a large winged-back seat. The screens on each monitor were blank.

"Control room?" Dan whispered.

"Let's see," Elspeth said quietly as she approached a terminal.

The keypad was built into the desk, a thing of lights and angled alloy. Next to each keyboard, there was a single blue button on an oval base. Elspeth's fingers alighted on it for a moment, before withdrawing.

"Best not press things before we know what they do, right?" she said.

"This whole thing is one big guessing game. Maybe we should just do it." Despite the bravado, Dan didn't seem that sure.

Elspeth looked up at the blank, steel walls and noted something about their surface. "What's that?"

Dan went to the spot where Elspeth indicated. At regular points, he observed that there was a barely discernible recess, a thin line that formed a rectangular shape above the terminal.

He went to each workstation and checked them in turn. "They all have one."

Elspeth looked from the blue button to the depressed rectangle. Her fingers returned to the plinth, hovering over the button.

"Time to take the plunge."

***

At the sound of growling behind her, Knowles moved quickly. Despite the discomfort emanating from the action, she rolled to her right and came up on one knee, swiping the rucksack from her back and brandishing the misshapen material like a sling. Time seemed to stand still, such was the sight waiting for her, and she took it in, as the roars and snarls from the dwelling where Sully was trapped with the hybrid continued to echo about the chamber.

There were three yetis all snarling at her; one was a few inches shorter than Sully, the other two no more than her height. The menace they exuded almost paralysed her with fear, but she'd been in situations such as this before, stand-offs were sometimes part of the mission, and she was under no misconceptions that had these creatures wanted to do so, they could have torn her to pieces before she'd even known they were there.

Knowles placed her bag on the floor, and cast her eyes down, while raising her palms up; the classic subjugation stance. The growls dropped to mere hisses as she made her intentions clear.

Without looking up, and without knowing if these incredible beasts could comprehend, Knowles spoke. "My friend is hurt, in trouble. Can you help him?"

She gestured to the archway where haphazard shapes flickered in the creamy silver light as Sully and the hybrid did battle.

The bigger of the three yetis broke free of the group and stormed over the dwelling. Knowles watched it go, its movements powerful but there was a poise to its gait, the way the hips swayed, the way it carried itself as it moved. The twin mounds on the chest.

Female, Knowles thought. *Trust a woman to come along and sort out the shit.*

Sure enough, the yeti stepped up to the archway. She looked back, barking at her companions who bounded over to her, leaving Knowles forgotten in the cavern.

Without invitation, the three creatures jumped into the chamber and Knowles ran over as all hell broke loose.

As Knowles gripped the rough edges of the doorframe, she witnessed wholesale carnage. The three newcomers had already grabbed at Sully and wrestled him away from the clutches of the hybrid. Not realising they were new-found allies, Sully made a feeble attempt to resist them, but it was to no avail as they swatted away his arms, held them, and hauled him free. His leg was now dragging behind him, the hybrid's lower limb still sticking out of the furred thigh, the hair matted with dark crimson. Beyond Sully the hybrid was now having to fend off a multiple, complex assault, orchestrated by the female yeti.

One of the smaller yetis had leapt upon the domed abdomen, grasping at thick, spiny hairs for purchase as it balled its right fist and began pounding down, the sickening sound of something cracking crossed the dwelling. Suddenly, with a pop, the fist punched through the abdomen and gouts of green fluid began arcing through the air, splattering the yeti as it jumped clear.

The hybrid let go a huge roar, but the assault did not stop. The second small yeti ran and then dived to the floor, rolling up into a ball, its knees beneath its chin, looking almost comical.

The creature rolled underneath the hybrid, keeping free of the legs seeking to trample it, passing the cephalothorax and stopping at the pedicel, where the yeti then went to all fours and with one mighty heave flipped the hybrid onto its back, the green ooze slopping out onto the floor of the dwelling like the world's largest gooseberry smoothie. In the commotion, the yeti beneath the hybrid leapt clear with a mighty roar of triumph.

The hybrid thrashed around, trying desperately to push itself upright, but all three yetis were now upon it, tearing at the exposed underbelly, ripping off legs like a malicious, bored child during summer vacation, not caring for their own safety, just determined to end this beast and bask in the glory of the vanquished.

Knowles went to Sully, checking him over. He put a great hand on her shoulder. "Sully good."

She looked him over. "You're bleeding like a stuck pig. We've got to get you out of here."

"Sully not a pig."

She smiled sadly. "Yeah, yeah. I know, lost in translation."

They both looked over at the hybrid and their savage cavalry. The yetis were standing over the mangled creature, the female holding Sully's club. The hybrid's simian face was now slack, life ebbing away as they all watched. Knowles could see all rage had fallen away from them; their stance appeared more rueful than victorious. The female knelt beside the hybrid, and without warning clamped her hands about its head and twisted it, snapping its neck in an instant.

The female looked over at Sully who nodded and in those few seconds, Knowles knew they had exchanged more than she could ever understand. But then the yeti spoke to Sully and Knowles wasn't surprised to find she understood the words.

"Mate?" she said, pointing at Knowles.

Sully winced when he tried to stifle a laugh. "No."

"Why she here?"

Sully was thoughtful. Then said, "Friend."

Knowles leaned in to him to show the mutuality of his statement.

She addressed the yeti standing across the dwelling. "Yes, I'm his friend and he's hurt. Can you help?"

The female tilted her head and considered Knowles. She nodded and addressed the two smaller yetis. "Maya, Mlaa, go, cubs. Find *lifeblood*. In the caves, in the pools."

One of the yetis - another female, Knowles noted - grabbed a discarded bowl from the floor and bounded off, past Knowles and Sully, and out into the cavern. The second yeti followed her. The sound of their scampering feet reverberated about them all.

Knowles pointed after them. "Cubs?"

"Cubs," the yeti said. Her shoulder slumped.

"And their father?" Knowles asked.

The female bowed her head. "Father dead. Many moons past."

Knowles didn't try to stop her sigh. Here was a tale of another being lost to the invaders. Another loved one to mourn.

CHAPTER EIGHT

In the depths of the earth, an incredible structure of blue-grey alloy merged with a chamber of magma and lava. Where metal met rock, a seal of thick glass highlighted the type of science, the type of ferocity, that had forced these two elements together, conjoining them for centuries. The machine was ovoid, and a series of pipes and tendrils rose from it, making the whole thing look as though a mechanical spider was climbing up the rockface.

Inside this edifice, there was a laboratory, and in this place of glass, and steel and science, a VDU displayed a series of bright yellow dots on a maze of green concentric lines. The console housing the screen was made of a deep blue metal and ornamented with aqua and purple lights; the tiny, gaudy sparkles reflected in huge, lidless eyes.

The creature scrutinising the output on the screen did so with a face incapable of demonstrating emotion. Its grey skin was pulled taut by high cheekbones, its mouth little more than a slit, framed by fat, blue lips.

While his countenance was incapable of expressing emotion, *Olok Chiblice* was not beyond the concept, nor its influences. Within him, sentiment - usually self-serving - burned like the brightest star in the heavens, like the very star orbited by his distant home planet, a home he had not seen for quite some time.

Olok reached up with long, stick-thin fingers, the skin of his hand so grey it was almost translucent. He pressed one of the aqua lights and the image on the screen changed. A small hiss came from his snout, a sign of disgust in his native language. The sound brought others to the screen, kindred that were equally reviled by the figures walking through the tunnels.

"They are vermin," Olok muttered. "A pestilence that should be liquidised, not studied."

A larger alien standing behind him shook its bulging bald head, the yellowed veins at its temples throbbing with fluid. "Be that as it may, Olok, our purpose here is clear. We are but employees doing the will of our clients. This you must keep in mind, always. The penalties for insurrection are severe."

"I am aware of such things, Administrator Druh," Olok said, his tone sharp even by the standards of his native language. "But we have seen how dangerous these creatures can be if left unchecked. Do I need to remind you of *recent events*?"

"The base?" Druh said. "A mere contractual blip, Chief Scientist. One of which I have no concerns, and as Administrator of this contract, my assurance should be enough for you. We have at least been able to test the design of the war machines in rudimentary combat. Field tests are a bonus. Allowing humans into a meaningless tributary also gives us opportunity to study from afar, am I correct?"

"Under normal circumstances," Olok grumbled.

The two aliens were colleagues of long standing, so was the animosity between them. An Administrator with concerns for the completion of their project balanced against a Chief Scientist so maverick he'd experiment on his own staff if he thought he could get this infernal assignment over with and go back home.

Druh shifted his bulk; a silver robe did its best to hide a bulbous stomach. "Your priorities lie beyond science it seems, Olok. *The Balon Co-Operative* did not gain our reputation in the universe by being 'normal'. Besides, we still have the *containment protocol*. The *nanofly* net in the atmosphere is our contingency. This planet can be held in stasis if there is a need. Not that I expect a scenario where that will ever occur."

Olok swivelled on his chair to look up at the mass standing over him. "My priorities are clear. The fact that we have such a protocol proves there is a risk, Druh. Why risk our ship bringing these things into the labyrinth?"

The Administrator stepped back, his arms wide with disbelief. "Are you not a scientist, Olok? Research requires us to have contact with the lifeforms of this world. Establish their weaknesses and from such knowledge create something unique in the universe. That is what we are contracted to achieve. As you well know."

Olok scoffed. "We have already established that humans are physiologically weak. They cannot take the scientific trauma of experimentation. Take that *thing* in the containment chamber for example.

An exercise in uselessness. I feel we can learn nothing more from their kind. Left to their own devices, these animals will destroy themselves."

Druh leaned uncomfortably close as he took in the images on the monitor. "Yes, and their world with them. And that cannot be allowed to happen. Our clients are quite clear about that, Olok. It is such things that will infringe contracts, damage reputations. Things that will bring consequences. For all of us."

Olok pushed his chair back, nudging Druh's overweight stomach, forcing him to step away.

"So, what do you propose?"

Druh spoke as softly as their coarse intonation would allow. "As Administrator, the last thing I intend to do is allow these creatures to undermine our project, Olok."

"So, what *is* your recommendation, Administrator?"

Druh moved towards a set of arched doors, their surfaces gleaming in the overhead lamps.

"Let them go where we *allow* them to go, just as they have up to this point. Then, we shall establish what our clients want done with them."

"Then what?" Olok pressed.

"We will fulfil whatever amendments are made to our contract. And terminate what is no longer required."

"Very well." Olok turned off the screen.

But, even though the images on the VDU had disappeared, his reservations had not.

***

In the tunnel system, the cubs went in search of Lifeblood. They traversed the narrow passages, climbing into several small spaces until another cavern yawned before them. Mala went to step forwards, but his sister placed a paw on his arm.

"You go wrong way, Mala. Your brain thick, like goat dung."

"You smell like goat dung, Mlaa."

The two cubs grunted with laughter, their guffaws rumbling around the cavern. The murky light about them was, as always, given off from a small pool of Lifeblood, nestled in a hollow; its surface seemed to pulsate as they approached, the light coming off of it, unstable.

Mlaa pointed at the pool. "Lifeblood better in next cave."

"Lifeblood same in every cave," Mala countered.

"Better colour in next cave. Make more light. Stronger."

Mala considered his sister-cub, his eyes squinting with thought. "We go next cave. Lifeblood stronger."

"You listen to sister. Brain not goat dung."

He bowed his head in thanks, but it was premature when she added, "Brain soft like gull-splat."

With that she ran off laughing again and Mala playfully chased after her. They went left, skirting the edges of the cavern.

As cubs they were used to the mountain and its secrets. Ever since they could remember, its caves and tunnels had kept them safe. From the earliest days, Mamma had ensured that they understood this murky place was not only their home, but the only way they could survive the invaders, and the terrible things that they did to those who were captured.

Mala loved the freedom of the open air, roaming the slopes whenever the chance arose, usually when the weather was too bad for humans to be on the mountain with their picture devices. Sometimes he had fun by deliberately leaving footprints for them to find in the freshly fallen snow.

Deeper into the cavern they came to an opening in the ragged wall. The hole was tinged with soft light and the gnarled floor had a gently rising gradient.

Mala went first, his great snout tracking any ill scent in the heavy air. After three long sniffs, he nodded, satisfied.

"We go on."

They continued, confident in their own skills. Their Momma was a strong female, her mate – their Dada – had perished when they were very small, killed by the sky people while hunting in the southerly tunnels. Without his protection, Mamma became warrior, teacher and carer; everything they knew had come from her drive to keep the family safe.

Powering up the slope, Mala found the walls and ceiling opening up into another vast opening a few hundred metres in. His sister was right, the Lifeblood was stronger here, he could see from the glow irradiating the cave, the light so bright it created a glimmering pillar that it splashed onto the high ceilings.

He shouldn't have been surprised, Mlaa was always right about such things. That was her nature, to think first and think well. He was different, perhaps because he was older (well, he was birthed a few minutes before his sister!), perhaps because his temperament was less refined. When he considered Mlaa's approach to life, her love of painting their adventures on the walls of their home, or telling stories after a good meal, he sometimes felt jealous, and then he'd feel bad. He wanted to be able to have the honour to protect the family and, as much as he honoured his Mamma, he yearned for his Dada's guidance on the warrior way.

Disturbing his thoughts, Mlaa scampered past him.

"Quick to find, slow to do, Brother!"

"You have the bowl, Sister."

Mlaa stooped, submerging the bowl into the glowing fluid. She peered into the light.

"Good and strong. Needed for bad wound."

"And good healing," Mala added.

Mlaa was thoughtful when she turned to him. "Will *he* be our Dada when he is healed?"

"No." His voice was gruff with annoyance.

"You don't want a Dada, Brother?" Mlaa said gently.

"Our Dada is gone."

"Many of our kind have gone. We need each other."

She stood and came over to him, the bowl secured by her big hands. "Is Mala good?"

"Yes," he said, but his smile was weak and there were tears in his eyes.

She carefully placed the bowl on a rocky ledge and hugged him to her. There, in the alien twilight, brother and sister sought some kind of Earthly peace.

***

In the milky half-light emanating from the subterranean lake, Bart assessed his makeshift treatment of Collins' wound. Both men had lost track as to how long they had been holed up in the cavern. Time was now a meaningless entity, countered only by their sense of urgency to get to more familiar surroundings.

"You think it'll work?" Collins asked, his query accompanied by a hiss of pain.

Bart peered at the wound-site. "It's double stitched, it'll hold as long as you don't put too much pressure on it."

"We can't just sit around. We have to get out of here," Collins said but made no attempt to act on his comments.

Bart looked about him. "Wherever 'here' is, Steve."

"Don't call me that, okay? 'Collins' or 'motherfucker' will do."

Bart nodded with a bemused smile. His companion's foibles were the least of his concerns right now.

"I'm going to see how the land lies, my friend. Then we can decide on what to do next, yes?"

"As long as the plan involves getting the hell out of here."

Bart stood. "Of course. But first we must establish where we can get *the hell* to, without putting us in more danger."

Collins remained quiet, a tacit agreement that Bart accepted instantly. He examined the locale without another word, his eyes following the edges of the lake, his mind trying to calculate the distances from the fluid perimeter to his current position. His best guess was at least five hundred metres to the farthest shoreline.

He went to walk off to his left and Collins' panicked voice came up to him. "Hey, where the hell you going? Don't just leave me here."

"That's not going to happen. I'm just looking for an exit, okay? I will be straight back. I promise."

"Yeah? Well, my experience of promises is they aren't worth Jack shit," Collins grumbled.

"Then let me prove you wrong," Bart said, continuing before Collins became too riled.

He scrambled over a cluster of rocks - the grit sharp against his palms, trying to ignore the dull ache in his ankle. He looked down and observed the fine particles, they were silver and glimmered with their own light. None of this made any sense, and he was fast becoming resigned to drawing a line under what he thought he knew and how things actually were in this subterranean mystery.

Stalagmites rose in huge columns ahead, their surfaces were multiple tributaries of creamy silver, the shadows they cast, deep and ominous.

Something stirred on the stale air. He held up a hand and felt the breeze coming at him. If there was any way out, he needed only to follow the rush of warm air to find it. Envigored, he pressed on, aware that he was leaving Collins further behind him than he would like, but without a sure-fire way out, it was pointless moving him on a fool's errand.

Bart edged his way around the stalagmites, heart racing, knowing that he was in no position to defend himself should those incredible creatures appear. He thought about the weaponry he'd seen take out the chopper, thought about the snarling snapping jaws, and considered those against the hunting knife he had strapped to his boot.

Pathetic didn't even make the cut.

Regardless of this, he knew their death would be pitifully slow if they were trapped in the cavern, even with the subterranean lake. Bart wasn't too sure if the water was safe to drink. As he'd said to Collins, its viscosity was a concern. It was difficult not to think of lifeboats packed with thirsty survivors floating on an ocean of water they were unable to drink. Madness would probably claim them before dehydration did.

Damn, it was getting difficult to stay positive, but it was a scientific dilemma, and it was in this realm he felt more at home. Science may have trapped them here, but it would ultimately define their rescue. He just had to find a way to balance the equation.

The uneven surface beneath his boots changed. Rather than the crunch of grit, there came the dull thud of rubber sole against metal. Bart looked down to see that he had stepped onto a slightly raised concourse leading off to a circular doorway. The entrance's circumference was smooth, too consistent to be natural, and Bart paused for a moment to assess how best to proceed.

Laughter from behind him made him spin, the guffaws bouncing around the cavern, distorting them into the sounds of madness. Bart tried to judge their direction, but he knew the source, there was only one other living entity down here with him, and that was Collins.

Hastily, he made his way back to his companion, and Bart was to realise Collins wasn't the only other living thing down here after all.

***

In the arboretum, Knowles looked at the female yeti sitting across from her. The atmosphere was sombre. Sully lay on his back, stock still, his leg raised on one of the chairs that they'd dragged from the dwelling. Knowles had used the strapping from her rucksack as a tourniquet, securing it high on his thigh, just above the wound. The hybrid's lower leg still skewered the limb, but Knowles had learned enough from the battlefield to know that it was better left in situ, as it would help stem the bleeding.

She tried to break the mood. "Do you have a name?"

"Maal," the yeti replied. She pointed at Knowles. "You?"

"Knowles." She patted her chest for emphasis.

71

Maal looked over at the entrance to the arboretum where her children had exited to find the substance they called *Lifeblood.*

It was a term Knowles had never heard before, but she was more than familiar with the silver liquid it referred to, an alien substance found in the walls of areas under extra-terrestrial influence. The precious fluid had healed her not too long ago, and Sully had been the saviour to introduce her to it. It was the only good thing the aliens had brought to her world.

Her heart was heavy as she looked at her friend, his stature somehow diminished by his pain.

"You care for him," Maal observed quietly.

"Yes. He saved my life."

"He saves more than that," Maal said cryptically.

"Huh?"

"Sully warrior like Maal."

Knowles acknowledged her with a smile. "You're a mother, too."

"Better warrior when Mamma. Give reason to live, to fight harder."

"I get that. So, your cubs, how old are they?"

Maal tilted her head in thought. "Two-hundred and thirty-five moons".

Based on the lunar calendar, Knowles did a quick calculation. *Nineteen years old*, she thought. Then, "They're twins."

Maal scrunched up her face as she tried to interpret the term. "Born same moon? Yes. Twins. Mala, he-cub. Mlaa, she-cub. Both strong. Near to the *Caalan*, naming ceremony. They receive name from Maal."

"Mala and Mlaa are not their names?" Knowles said, fascinated.

"No. They are *Gammala*, cub names. *Caalan* means they have adult name. Start family, receive honour."

"Only Maal can give them names?"

Maal nodded emphatically. "Only *Mamma*. Or *Mommash*, family member with high honour. Sully accepts his name from you. You are Mommash."

Knowles thought about this for a moment, the implication of Sully's words on the slope as he accepted the name she'd given him on a whim. It made her feel simultaneously privileged and ashamed. He deserved a better name, one that showed his proud nature and his incredible strength of will. Not a throwback to a fucking kid's movie.

A thought came to her. "What if names are not given?"

Maal's response was instant. "No moving on to *Thirsk*, high honour. Cub becomes outcast."

Knowles tried to make sense of it but gave up. "I don't understand."

Maal nodded. "No matter. This is our way."

There was no reproach in Maal's demeanour. Instead she merely stretched her shoulders and gave out a large yawn. Seconds later she sniffed the air and her muzzle drew back into a smile.

"Cubs return," she said before Knowles' ears picked up echoey footfalls coming from the arboretum entrance.

The cubs entered the arboretum, Mlaa's pace slow and cautious, her brother walking beside her.

Her moment with Maal now lost, Knowles looked at the cubs as they neared. Mlaa held the bowl, and it brimmed with shimmering liquid that threw silvery light into her face, turning it to a vista of alternating dark and creamy shadow.

Mlaa presented the bowl to Maal, both bowed their heads as though this was some form of ritual.

"Lifeblood, Mamma."

Maal took the bowl from her daughter. "Keep watch my cubs. Mamma do healing work."

In silence, Knowles watched; her concern betrayed by the deep lines in her face. Helpless and quietly dismayed, all she could do was wait.

CHAPTER NINE

Olok sat back in his hydration unit, the pool of yellowed plasma setting to work on his body. As he disappeared beneath the surface, deep pores unsealed in his skin, opening, and closing, like hundreds of tiny mouths gulping down vital nutrients.

He mulled over his recent discussion with Druh. The Administrator's comments about priorities were pointed and accurate. Olok craved to be back where he belonged, the cluster of stars beyond this universe where his family waited for him in stasis, waited for his return.

In his mind, he scoffed. Return? This was becoming more dream than an actuality. He was already overdue by a hundred Earth years. He was in quantum prison at the behest of their current clients. But this wasn't about science at all, was it? It was about fulfilling a contract from a race of people who wanted the strange and the eccentric. They wanted the *unique*.

Sometimes he enjoyed the challenges presented to him as Chief Scientist. He certainly enjoyed the prestige. But those moments were becoming few and far between. Not helped by Druh being committed to meeting their contract down to the final detail. And this meant exploring the kind of science that kept Olok on this infernal planet for multiple lifetimes.

Now the Administrator was adding the reckless nature of humans into the mix. Olok would have welcomed this had the project been nearing completion. But as it stood, humans in the labyrinth would be a distraction and risked causing the kind of damage that could keep him on this worthless planet for good.

He could not risk it. He *would not* risk it.

And, as he'd pointed out to Druh earlier, Olok had already tried human experimentation on an intrinsic level. The remnants of said experiment was now nothing more than a malformed effigy, kept alive by machines out of pure curiosity as to how resilient humans functioned on a cognitive level. So far this had yielded little more than endless screams coming through the brain-reading equipment.

So, Olok really could not see the point of tempting fate any further. And could not see why Druh would either. Druh was an Administrator and by design a cautious character. Perhaps it was a mere show of power, the Administrator flexing his status and reminding Olok of what could be lost if he failed to focus on the scientific task at hand.

As if he needed reminding!

Solving the puzzle meant getting back home, Olok was clear enough on that mandate. He simply was not prepared to accept human recklessness in the background. He already knew what he was going to do about it.

Like the physiological defence systems of organic life, the labyrinth had the means of eradicating infection. And Olok had the impetus to use them, with or without Druh's sanction.

The hydration tank was his only solace on this intrusive, primitive world, that and the occasional breakthrough with the science.

Sensing such thoughts were influencing his sense of peace, Olok tried to distract himself with images from home. The great oceans of Ceed'ar, the waters as yellow as sun-splashed deserts. Swimming deep, Reeka, his mate, and *spoolings* with him, relishing the intimacy psychic links provided in the viscous tide.

He felt himself become one with the hydration tank, his mind reaching the *neurofield*, the middle ground where minds could meet across galaxies. This was a safe space, a cushion to keep them all connected to the realities of travelling through time and space.

Like their influence throughout the galaxies, the dimensions in which they travelled as a species was vast and unfathomable. Devices such as this were intrinsic to their culture, the great oceans providing the resources to give them capacity to survive so far away from home.

"You are troubled." Reeka was in his mind.

"Yes. This world, this work. It is not worthy of my abilities."

Reeka's tone was as smooth as the fluid in which he drifted. "We are defined by our commitments, Husband. You know this."

"Yet I cannot accept it, Reeka. As my mate you can sense my unhappiness."

In his head, Reeka smiled, her eyes turning purple, the sign of sadness. Of understanding.

"And I embrace it, Husband. Our standing here is dependent on your duty. Would you have us without worth?"

"No." Olok bowed his head, submitting to the words of his spouse.

"Then let us talk of our life to come, Olok. Let us co-join in peace."

Their minds met and fused together. For the time he was in the hydration tank, Olok enjoyed the pleasures of love and union, making memories to keep him sane so many lightyears from home.

***

"Sonofabitch!" Collins hissed as he adjusted his position against the rocks. His wound burned like a brand.

In front of him, the lake shimmered, languid waves lapping at the shore. There was a rhythm to the sucking and slurping of the surf, he found himself mesmerised by it, soothing him as a lullaby would soothe a tired infant.

After a time, he really couldn't take his eyes away from the undulating water.

Collins allowed tranquillity to wash over him. After what seemed like an age of being in pain, it was such a relief. Yet he also felt the influence go deeper than the physical hurt in his lower back, he found the ongoing anxiety he carried with him for such a long time slip away too; anaesthetised by the lilting water.

To his own surprise, he found himself on his feet. He felt as though the lake was calling to him and the voice was that of his long-dead father. There was no question of how such a thing could be, Collins merely took this latest event as a new kind of truth, one where the fantastic had just as much legitimacy as normalcy.

Slowly, he dragged his boots across the uneven floor, his head tilted as he listened to his father's voice.

"I've missed you, son."

"Me, too, Dad." Collins was smiling but tears were running down his cheeks. "I can't believe you're here."

"Everything is possible, *Steve*. You just must believe. You just have to want it more than anything else in the world."

Collins looked about him. "Where are you? Can I see you?"

"I'm so proud of you, Steve. The man you've become. What you've achieved."

"Where are you, Dad?" Collins struggled to keep his voice calm. The desire to see his father was powering through him. He felt like an addict jittering over his next fix.

"Come to the edge of the water, Son. Then you'll see me."

"Do you promise?" Collins was no longer aware that he had adopted the voice of a small child. In his mind he was that young boy who had lost the man he held in such esteem, the man who he needed to impress for so long. It wasn't until that very moment he realised how much he needed his father's sanction, how much he craved it. The revelation almost took his breath away.

"Yes. Yes, I promise."

Dragging his sleeve across his face, Collins wiped away tears and snot. His heart was light, a sense of euphoria that threatened to make him scream out with joy. In his regressed mind, he held this in check, but in the cavern, he was laughing; loud and wanton, not caring who could hear.

He reached the shoreline, squatted down, the makeshift sutures tearing open and allowing fresh blood to pour down the seat of his fatigues. He was unaware of this, so besotted was he with an incredible sight beneath the surface of the water.

Like a mosquito trapped in amber, his father appeared petrified in the jaundiced water. His face looked up at Collins, the smile serene, his clothing moving gently in the current.

Without any sense of propulsion, Collins' father broke the surface, his face first, then his shoulders, then waist, rising from the lake as though on a hydraulic platform, until he stood on the surface, hands reaching for his son, beckoning him.

"Come to me, Steve. Join me."

The surge of love Collins felt made him gasp, the happiness: beyond repression. Holding out his hands, Collins sought out long lost contact, their fingers mere inches apart.

Somewhere in his mind, Collins could hear shouting and screaming, but it was distant, like an argument through plate-glass. So, he buried it in his psyche as he finally made contact. Images flashed through his brain, lived experiences feeling as though they were been dragged from his mind and the sensation was not pleasant. It was something else entirely.

It was absolute agony.

Something else changed, too. His father was gone, the stoic image replaced by something incomprehensible, something with tentacles and teeth, and black eyes devoid of mercy. Suckers bit into his clothing, tearing through them, multiple gnawing teeth that ate into his flesh, locking in place, never to let go.

Steve Collins finally found reality when he was lifted from the shore and held high above the luminous water. That reality came with blood and screams, and a cry of despair from far below.

***

Elspeth chewed her lip as her fingers hovered over the blue button.

"What are you waiting for?" Dan said, his voice tight with urgency. "Appleby could be in there."

"Maybe that's what I'm afraid of," she whispered.

"We have to know, one way or the other," Dan said, his tone conciliatory. "It's why we're here."

She nodded and her long fingers followed her command. The button depressed without sound. In an instant, the screen came alive, shivering with a kaleidoscopic static, and the panel in the wall above slid slowly to the left with a barely noticeable hum. A shaft of turquoise light was thrown across the room, casting a perfect sickly oblong against the opposite wall.

Elspeth and Dan peered through the panel, noting the glass barrier between them and the chamber behind it. To their surprise they saw forestry; large ferns and the base of giant tree trunks filling the space beyond the window, and the light was cast by a series of pools on the floor, all fringed with reeds and rushes.

Something moved, the foliage trembling under its touch. At first, neither could make sense of the shape, because the body was predominantly hidden by the flora and trees. The creature emerged without warning, giving out a soundless roar, fangs turned into gaudy spikes by the hideous lighting. Cold, feline eyes stared at them from the safety of the vegetation, indicating its wariness.

Slowly the beast crawled from its hiding place, the great paws digging into the soft detritus, vicious claws puncturing the foliage with each step. The face was mottled, the mouth pulled back into an infinite snarl.

"Snow leopard," Elspeth said.

Dan pressed his face against the glass. "What is this, a fucking zoo?"

"Just be careful," she murmured. A small bleep had her looking down at the terminal screen which had now come to life. There was an image on there, a 3-D model of a creature she thought impossible. She could see the leopard shape, the markings and colouring as she'd expect from watching many National Geographic reruns, but there was something significantly wrong with the overall picture.

Dan pre-empted her thoughts. "Jesus Christ. Are you seeing this?"

He wasn't looking at the screen, his eyes remained fixed and wide, peering through the window. Elspeth joined him, and the creature came into view, the leopard crawling on its stomach, but behind it came the slithering body of a snake, the segments arched and muscular, the skin twinkling like asphalt after rain.

They watched as the leopard stepped and glided free of the forest. A beast as pathetic as it was astonishing, and Elspeth was surprised to find a tear fall down her cheek.

"Who the hell did this?" Dan seethed.

Elspeth was more measured in her response. "You *know* who. The question is *why*."

"Maybe there isn't any 'why'. Maybe they're just intergalactic psychopaths who get a kick out of fucking up this planet."

Elspeth said nothing, choosing instead to hit the blue button again, shutting the lid on this current version of Pandora's Box. As soon as the panel closed, the image on the screen disappeared, making her immediately consider what was behind the other terminals. She went to the next and sat down at the workstation.

"Do you really need to see anything else?" Dan asked.

"I need to understand it."

"You're sick, Elspeth." His voice was flat, as though he didn't honestly believe his statement.

She ran her fingers through her fiery hair. "If we know what's going on then maybe we can use it to our advantage somehow. You must see that?"

"Yeah. I get it." He didn't sound happy with his assessment. "Go on. Try another."

Another workstation, another button. The panel pulled back and this time the light was green and watery as they looked upon a tank of the kind usually found in a large aquarium. Dan held his breath as dark shadows moved through the fluid seascape.

He scrunched up his face as he saw the proximity of one panel to the next. They were separated by mere feet. "How can a forest be next to an ocean?"

Elspeth rubbed her chin. "How can a leopard be spliced to a snake? This whole thing is a contradiction."

"What you call contradiction, I call bullshit," he muttered as Elspeth watched the terminal fulfil its function and bring the screen to life.

She didn't recognise the creature rotating on the VDU. "This is something new. Something not from our world."

Humanoid and covered with oily green scales, it had large silver eyes on the side of a coned head, and both feet and hands were webbed. There were gills at the slender neck, and the mouth was puffed up with rubbery, red lips.

"Looks like someone put their make-up on in the dark," Dan said.

They turned their eyes back to the tank as something loomed out of the dark waters at speed. It struck the glass with incredible force, rattling the pane in its frame. Elspeth jumped back and Dan lifted his assault rifle.

By the time they'd composed themselves, they saw only blurred images of the creature swimming away and back into the murk.

Dan laughed in relief. "Jesus. I thought that thing was coming through."

But Elspeth did not share the good humour. "Better close the panel. The water pressure in that tank is going to be huge."

She got as far as sitting down at the terminal when another huge thud filled the room; this time there was a hiss as a diagonal crack sliced through the pane, and liquid fizzed through.

"We need to get the hell out of here!" Dan prepared his rifle and Elspeth drew her sidearm.

They moved away from the terminal, heading further into the room, their intention to put some distance between them and the creature determined to break free of its enforced habitat.

As Elspeth had feared, the glass gave way under the pressure. They ran, and the surge of water smashed through the room, toppling chairs, and causing the terminals to fizz and spark. The wave took Elspeth and Dan off their feet, dumping them into the churning water, filling their mouths with vile, sickly sweet fluid, making them gag and flounder.

Dan tried to stand, but the water was slippery, as though he'd stepped in motor oil. He slapped a palm against the wall and cried out in anger and frustration as the rifle slipped from his grasp and was lost to the grimy water. Then, something else was in the room with them, something that mewled like an irritated rat, and a shape rose from the roiling liquid.

If this creature had appeared formidable behind a glass screen, standing before them, glistening and its juddering body giving off blubbery noises, it was a thing of bizarre horror.

Dan searched frantically for his rifle; the murky, churning water still pouring through the window making the task beyond difficult.

"Shoot it, Elspeth! For Christ's sake, shoot the fucking thing!"

But Elspeth was braced against the wall, shoulder taking her weight, water slopping around her thighs and steadily climbing. She'd raised the Glock, but it seemed to weigh three times what it had the last time she'd drawn it. The weapon trembled in her hands, the creature stared back at her, seemingly undeterred by the gun trained on it. She watched in macabre fascination as the creature closed off its gills, each one snapping shut with a wet slap. She felt her stomach lurch.

It sloshed forwards through the water, towards Dan, and this ended her paralysis. She opened fire, putting three rounds into the chest. Blue fluid smattered its torso and it gave out a watery cry, the impact pushing it backwards. But in seconds it was launching itself through the air, like a cat pouncing on a wayward rodent caught wandering through its domain.

The thing bowled Dan out of the way, sending him under the water, and lashed out at Elspeth, catching her on the abdomen, lifting her high and she came down on a terminal, her coccyx smashing into the workstation, sending a flair of pain down both her legs, and they gave way, pitching her into the vile fluid.

In the melee, she lost the gun, fought for breath, tried to push through the numbness in her thighs. Then something had her about the throat, a scaly forearm clamping onto her, pulling her backwards, a bright, singing pain in her right shoulder telling her that this thing had sharp teeth. She screamed, water gushing from her throat, the sound a hideous blend of forced air and fluid.

Her vision fogged, life draining away from her, she could feel the warmth of her own blood flowing upon her face. From far away she heard dull, booming thuds, the slippery surface beneath her shook, and then the incredible rendering of metal.

She was free!

Suddenly and inexplicably she no longer had the crushing arm about her throat, the teeth biting down on her shoulder parted, almost making her pass out as the pressure was released.

She was shoved forwards, clearing the water briefly, her injured shoulder striking the wall, making her scream in pain.

Before she could go under, hands grabbed at her again, and she found a new surge of vigour, to fight, to live. Her uninjured arm came up to take a swipe at her attacker, but something came to her through the din.

Dan's voice was loud and bristling with fear. "Just keep going, Elspeth. Keep going and don't stop."

She succumbed. Allowing him to propel her onwards, towards the exit at the far end of the room.

They both staggered towards the door, holding onto each other, keeping their chances of staying alive in their grasp. Dan punched the buttons and the oval door lifted, the water at their waist flowing through. They backed up, staring down at the corridor and Elspeth gasped at the sight they were leaving behind.

"What did you do?" she whispered, her incredulity momentarily overriding the pain.

"Got us some help."

Back down the short corridor, the *aquabeast* was embroiled in a battle with the creature from the forest. The two kaiju fought with incredible savagery, blood flowed from claws and teeth, terminals were sent smashing into walls, the scene quickly becoming one of water and carnage.

Mercifully, the doors closed on the brutal image. Seconds later, Elspeth collapsed.

CHAPTER TEN

Maal and her cubs had moved Sully to another, less spacious dwelling, their combined might hefting him, and carrying his weight with awkward yet effective efficiency. Knowles could only walk on behind, carrying the precious bowl of Lifeblood, held out before her like Oliver on his way to ask Mr Bumble for more gruel.

They had placed Sully on a table in the central living area. Throughout the process, Knowles could hear his supressed grunts of pain, and each one put an ache in her heart. This was a being of immense pride, a warrior, and she knew such help would not sit comfortably with him.

Maal gestured for Knowles to approach. "Healing is the duty of the *Mommash*."

Uncertain, Knowles looked questioningly at Maal.

"Sully accepted the name you gave," she explained. "You are responsible, to keep him safe, protect him at his time of need."

"I ain't too sure how I feel about that," Knowles said, placing the bowl on a nearby chair. "I can't even look after myself most of the time."

Maal looked intensely at Knowles. "There is strength in the bond between *Mommash* and Gammala. A power that lives beyond life."

Knowles could feel the stirring emotion in her heart. Maal was not wrong. Knowles' connection to Sully was growing in ways she could not explain. These days she'd seen so many incredible things, she'd learned quickly not to question it. But she fell short of giving it a name, embracing it for what it was, because to do that would mean fostering the feeling, making an attachment to something that could be lost at any point beneath this infernal mountain.

She was no coward on the field of battle, she'd take a bullet for anyone to keep them safe, but she never allowed herself to dig into the *why-for* of her actions, merely ascribing it to a determination to keep the mission on track.

The truth was even easier; emotions meant a kind of pain that put fear into her belly, and the vulnerability this evoked was something akin to poison.

Beside her, Sully lay in a fitful sleep. There were beads of sweat on his heavy brow, and his lips moved, the murmurs that came from them were indecipherable, even for the translator.

"Come, Knowles," Maal said, taking hold of the spider's leg embedded into Sully's thigh. "He will need your comfort."

Knowles placed a hand on Sully's head, playing with the fur on his crown. She should have felt awkward but did not. In fact, to not do so would have felt wrong, somehow she knew it, just as she somehow knew that these moments, no matter how things transpired, would cement their bond beyond that of brothers in arms; they were to become family.

In her head, she was back home and in her early teens, lying in her bed, underneath the duvet, after yet another scrape with the local constabulary, and the inevitable row with her mother. This was two years before her parent's divorce and delinquency really ramped up to the point where the army became her only out.

Gloria Knowles, her mother, had looked at her on that night, her face holding the quiet frustration that was so prevalent after all the shouting had moved on.

"You know, Clarice," her mother had said, "you'll never understand the love between a mother and her children until you become a mother yourself. There is a power there that you will never be able to fathom but you will embrace it, and you won't want it to end."

At the time, a young Knowles had heard these words through her duvet, rolling her eyes in disbelief and anger. But now, as she comforted Sully, part of her embraced the concept of unconditional love, the emotional aspect, the bond between family that stood all the assaults life could throw at it.

"We begin," Maal whispered. "Ready?"

"Sorry. Just thinking."

"Think later."

Knowles nodded as Mala took hold of Sully's right wrist and Mlaa, the left. Placing her mouth next to his ear, Knowles spoke softly.

"Just relax, big fella. We're all here for you, okay? *I'm* here for you."

If there was any kind of ceremony attached to the moment, it didn't extend to the procedure. Without any count-in, Maal yanked the spider limb free and the room echoed with a squelch and the agonised cry from Sully. He raised his head and shoulders from the table, his powerful arms lifting Mala and Mlaa from their feet for a few seconds, but they held on, extending his limbs so they could add effective counterweight.

Head falling back, he groaned loud and long before slipping back into unconsciousness. Blood flowed from the wound and Maal allowed it to come, watching it pool on the table and pour in threads to the floor.

"Hey," Knowles said standing. "He's bleeding out!"

"Wait," Maal said. It wasn't a request.

"God damn it," Knowles said, moving forward. Maal placed a hand on her chest. It was like running into a wall.

"We must let any poison flow from the wound," Maal said, not unkindly. After what seemed like a lifetime she pointed to the bowl. "Lifeblood, now!"

As quickly as she could, Knowles picked up the bowl, some of the silvery liquid slopping onto her fingers, putting a pleasant warmth there, as though slipping on a pair of soft, heated mittens.

She took the bowl over to the table.

Maal indicated the wound on Sully's thigh. It was approximately ten inches in diameter and bubbled with thick blood. It gave off a faint odour, the beginnings of infection, and Knowles realised that Maal had been right to allow the period of bloodletting.

Carefully she poured the shimmering liquid into the wound and steam rose as it made contact, filling in the hole, sinking into it, and all the time the incredulity on Knowles' face as tissue and vessels knitted back together. The wound began to shrink, so too did Sully's fever break, and his muttering faded. His countenance became passive, his breathing slow and steady, as though he was in a deep, peaceful sleep.

Maal removed the tourniquet from Sully's thigh, throwing it to the floor. "Now he must rest. Come."

She stood and ambled across the dwelling, to an area piled with furs. There was a wall nearby, the surface buffed smooth. Maal pushed at it and an oval section rotated 180 degrees until there was a series of shelves protruding out from the wall. On these shelves were large stone storage jars, and Maal began taking them down, sniffing at the contents once she'd removed their stone lids.

"Do you live here?" Knowles said.

"No. These dwellings old. Tribe gone."

"Because of the aliens?"

Knowles saw Maal frown, unsure of her words. She jabbed a finger to the ceiling and then used a flat palm to imitate a spacecraft landing.

"Sky people?" Maal said.

"Yeah. Sky people."

"Yes. They drive tribes away. Kill those who stayed."

Maal called her cubs to her. Mlaa and Mala helped retrieve the pots she'd chosen from the shelf. They took them to the heap of pelts and furs, placing them down carefully on the floor.

"Where is your home?" Knowles asked.

"No home. We move."

Knowles took a moment for her brain to translate. "You mean you move around?"

Maal nodded. "Stay no place long. Keeps us alive. Bad things live under the mountain. Some the sky people brought with them. Others, they made."

Maal approached a spot on the floor. Knowles could see there was a square with a small metal eyelet into which Maal hooked her index finger and pulled up. The stone lifted free to reveal a small pit.

"We cook here," Maal explained. "Food stale but good. Came here last time, five moons ago."

Knowles understood. Maal and her cubs roamed free in the labyrinth, setting up waystations on their travels; just like the Kochi nomads Knowles herself had met in Northern Afghanistan. She watched as Mala and Mlaa pulled clumps of fur from their forearms and piled the mounds into the pit to form basic kindling. From another wall compartment, Maal pulled chunks of wood and a piece of flint.

The large yeti got to her all fours and began chipping at the stone about the pit and the sparks were bright, silent explosions in the muted light. After several attempts the fur caught and Maal breathed life into the fledgling fire, until the flames danced happily in the gloom.

"We make broth, make Sully strong again."

Knowles was suddenly humbled. "Thank you for helping us."

Bowing her head, Maal gave Knowles a smile. "Sully would die. You would be lost."

"Yeah. You got that right," Knowles conceded.

"Why are you here?" Maal asked.

This was a question that was always going to be strange to answer. The realities were based on extreme human emotions, but it was difficult to avoid being honest. Subterfuge had no place here; it had cost them all so much already.

"Shame steals your words," Maal said softly as she placed a pot onto the firepit. "Revenge hardens the heart."

"I guess so. But yeah, I'm here for revenge. I want the sky people off our planet. I want them to stop hurting people."

"Not only people," Maal reminded her.

"No." She looked over at Sully. "No, not just people. I know they killed a lot of your tribes. Under the other mountain, Sully showed me the drawings. On the walls?"

Maal stirred the soup. "Stories are truth, keep tribes alive."

"Like memories?"

"Yes."

"Why don't you come with us?" Knowles suggested.

Maal pointed to her cubs. There was no other explanation required; staying alive was more important, that was clear to Knowles. In that moment she considered her own position. Maybe she should just accept what was and go deep into the mountains, perhaps her and Sully could join with Maal and her cubs, becoming one tribe.

Then the irritation kicked in; she was running away from her duty to *her* people, hiding in the shadows while some creatures from outer space played god with the entire planet. This was what it truly came down to, revenge was the fuel, but survival was the machine that would see her wipe those bastards from the face of this mountain. Or die trying.

Lost to her thoughts, Knowles let the warmth of the firepit take her away for a while. The smoke rose from the cooking area, finding its way to the ceiling where it was whipped away through a natural vent like some invisible chimney flue, the crackles from the flames giving the dwelling a relaxing ambience.

Respite amongst the chaos.

***

Bart watched in powerless horror as the creature's thrashing body turned the lake into broiling havoc. He could see Collins held high in one of the beast's thick tentacles, its huge black eyes unfathomable.

Self-preservation tried to hold Bart back, but he pushed through it, determined to come to Collins' aid. Even as he crossed the chamber, he could see the futility of his attempts at rescue, compounded further by his limited weaponry. The creature had firm hold of his colleague, blood poured from the many wounds inflicted by the tentacles.

Collins' scream was seemingly endless, rising in pitch as the lake-beast began to constrict its limbs. There were pops and cracks as bones shattered, and Bart wept as he saw the head explode under the pressure, a fountain of gore spiralling upwards like foaming champagne from an uncorked bottle.

No celebrations here, though. Just pain and disgust and hopelessness. These things had Bart reeling away from the sight of Collins' broken body as it was dragged beneath the waters, the thick liquid slopping into the air and back down, gloopy and stained with blood.

Still weeping, Bart scrambled behind the stalagmite towers, leaning against them as he battled with his senses. Yes, he was crying, but he also beat his fist angrily against the smooth columns, the pain bringing him back into focus.

This place could easily be hell. But it was a hell that belonged to another realm, another world. There was no denying it, no way of fooling himself otherwise. To do so would have him at the bottom of the lake, crushed in the coiled limbs of the great beast.

Now that the commotion had died down, Bart found the silence oppressive, the sheer size of the cavern adding to, rather than muting, the feeling. He took in deep breaths to clear his head, deciding to go with his original plan and follow the source of the breeze. At once he questioned this, the scientist within him becoming more obstacle than ally.

Why are you going that way, Bart? Do you want to die?

The other way leads to the lake. And the thing that took Collins looks like it will need more than one man to satisfy its appetite.

But there will be creatures on the other side of the doorway. You're dead either way.

No!

Why?

Because ...

Because?

Because those creatures have machines. Because we can use them to escape!

He made his peace with his debating brain. He had no choice and he knew it. The only way out of this mountain was to find a machine that could do it for him. What that would look like and how it worked didn't really matter to him at that juncture. All he needed was hope, just like his momma always said. Hope and faith.

He stepped back onto the concourse, painfully aware that all that remained of his kit lay where Collins had succumbed to the beast. All he had was the knife and a layer of damp clothing between him and freezing to death once he got topside. He pushed the thoughts away; his drive now was to survive on a minute-by-minute basis.

The concourse ran for two hundred yards before it gave out to the doorway. As the portal became clearer, Bart could see strange markings around the frame. There was no saddle where it met the floor, the concourse appeared to just go straight through it as though it didn't exist at all. The surface of the door was all too familiar, a yellow viscous substance, like a blister turning bad.

The memory of Collins' demise wasn't too far away, and Bart silenced it by putting the sharp edge of his hunting knife across his forearm, the slicing pain keeping him focused. He paused at the threshold and took a breath before stepping inside. The blister offered token resistance before allowing him through, his face feeling warm as the skein washed over it.

On the other side was an oval antechamber, but this didn't consist of rock. The elliptical walls were smooth alloy, and, in places, lines of blue lights riveted the structure together. There was a strange taint to the air, but Bart was able to breathe as normal, without an adverse reaction.

Beyond the antechamber, he could see another spherical doorway. He moved towards it, keen to put distance between him and the cavern housing the lake and its deadly, murderous occupant.

Built into the frame, a small keypad formed an upright diamond-shape with the apex and nadir, intersected halfway by a horizontal, luminous blue strip. Scattered around the steel door, lights twinkled with various hues.

He tentatively pressed the top triangle. Without a sound, the steel door opened slowly in the archway, allowing him access to a compact space made of the same metal alloy as the antechamber.

Bart paused on the threshold. "An elevator. But to where?"

He stepped inside and looked at the control panel in the metal walls, the configuration identical to that outside.

"Guess I'm going to find out soon enough," he said, hitting the triangle and the door slid shut. He almost waited for terrible Muzak to pipe into the car, anything to normalise the insanity going on all around him.

He felt the car move, its direction barely perceptible, but enough to tell him he wasn't going up or down. Instead he was going diagonally and upwards, as though the car was resting on an escalator. He mused that, when the doors opened, he'd find himself in Diagon Alley from Harry Potter. He could sure do with access to some powerful magic right now.

The moment made him think about the stories his parents used to tell about his grandmother and her magic rituals. He shelved these immediately. There was no time for rumination and self-pity. He had to ride the elevator into the unknown, destination could-be-anywhere, and deal with whatever greeted him when those doors did finally open.

He held the knife firmly in his hand, trying not to succumb to the feeling that, all in all, his odds of fending off an attack were weighted in favour of his potential opponent.

He pressed on regardless.

***

Olok sat in his lab, his miserable demeanour unsettling all those about him. The laboratory was his only vestige, the only true evidence that he was, above all, a scientist.

If his superiors had their way, he'd be spending his entire life away from his family, splicing together divergent species, using crude mechanics to create bastardisations of genus, no more than a child building corrupt toys.

To most of the known galaxy their kind were already referred to as 'Splicers'. To Administrators like Druh this was a derogatory name, demeaning of the service *The Balon Co-operative* provided for their elite clientele. But to Olok the term was apt and, above all, accurate.

Yes, the demand for hybrid gene-tech was prevalent enough for it to be a significant slice of Balon income. But it was also considered fundamentally unethical, hence having to timeslip to alternate universes to carry out such projects, away from prying eyes. All in all, splicing was proving positive for business, yet dreary for science.

A lab-tech sidled up to him, a tablet in his hand. He waited patiently for Olok to acknowledge his presence.

"What is it?" Olok hissed impatiently.

"We have a breach, Chief Scientist."

"Where?"

"Containment chamber five," the lab-tech replied carefully.

"And what are you doing about it?"

After a pause, the lab-tech said, "Telling *you*, Olok?"

Muttering, Olok went over to the main console, where an operative sat pushing buttons for no apparent reason other than to look busy.

Part of Olok was riled, not because his reverie about home had been interrupted, but because humans in the containment chamber was not something he'd desired, and certainly not anticipated in his counter measures. In fact, he wasn't quite sure just how they'd been able to get in there without his influence. The whole thing was one huge irritant.

"Activate sensors in containment chamber five," Olok demanded.

"The sensors are damaged," the operative said bluntly after consulting his monitor.

"How?"

"The chamber has flooded."

Olok snorted with anger. "Am I the only one with any kind of brain? Get a unit down there. Maintenance and a suppression team."

"Suppression team?" the operative quizzed.

"Yes. Unless you want the maintenance team to be eaten alive?"

"Oh. Of course, Chief Scientist."

"And get me Druh. This mess is going to need administration."

"You want Druh at the containment chamber?" the operative said with as much of a frown its face could manage.

Olok sighed and signalled for one of the guards standing at the entrance gate to come over. The warrior was large and carried with him a confidence reflective of his standing.

"Yes, Olok?" the guard said.

"Give me your arc-pistol."

"Arc-pistol?" the guard said.

"Yes, yes. Your weapon - give it to me," Olok confirmed.

"Very well." Baffled, the guard unholstered the pistol, and handed it over.

With one swift action, Olok turned and shot the troublesome operative in the back, the single blast from the arc-pistol sending blood and sparks into the air. The operative's body slumped and then slid onto the floor as all in the room looked on.

Olok handed the arc-pistol back to the guard. "My apologies. But he was simply too stupid to live."

With that, Olok turned and left the laboratory, his fury still hot enough to have him punching the lab tech on the way out.

***

In the twilight of the Elder dwelling, the fallen hybrid lay motionless, a memorial to a terrible kind of science. The carcass had a pelt thrown over the face of the yeti, a token attempt by Knowles to afford the creature beneath at least some dignity in death.

The air about the dwelling was perfumed by the metallic taint of stale blood. There was a sudden noise. It was tiny and inconsequential, a cracking sound coming from the hybrid's ruined abdomen.

In one area, no more than a few centimetres in diameter, a patch of skin began pulsating, its surface thumping upwards, forming a blister. Within the translucent dome, something shuddered, pressing against walls of tissue until they burst, allowing the emergent drone to rise from a pool of clear, gelatinous fluid.

It was a delicate structure, legs and wings that moved without sound as it took flight. Like the being that had played host, the tech was not of this Earth, but its purpose was certainly of consequence to the native inhabitants nearby.

The drone left the dwelling and its sensors sought out the life forms in the area. As it moved through the air, the silver body changed to reflect the deep, gloomy browns of its surroundings.

Slowly, silently, the drone flew towards the sounds emanating from the dwelling where Sully was receiving treatment.

And, unknown to anyone inside, the chameleon fulfilled its purpose.

CHAPTER ELEVEN

Olok ruminated in his quarters. Sitting over a steaming vase of blue liquid, he considered his discussion with Reeka, his spouse, and his responsibility to protect the family's reputation. She was right, of course. His frustrations were born out of a need to get back to her, and to rush things would risk all he cared for, all he held in esteem.

A harsh buzzing interrupted his thoughts, making his foul mood even more sour.

"Go away."

"Chief Scientist, I have news from a hybrid reconnaissance drone." The voice through the intercom was timid, hesitant.

"Can I not even have a vase of *teavaal* in peace?" he muttered. "Enter."

A door on the far side of the room skimmed open and a male laboratory operative stood on the threshold. He clutched a transparent rectangle of glass to the chest of his lab-smock.

Olok held up his hands in despair. "Come on, come on. Don't dither, I haven't got all day."

The operative shuffled in, head bowed, a sign of reverence in the presence of high office. He pulled up short and without looking up offered the glass pane to Olok.

"Data from a drone in sector eight, Chief Scientist."

Olok tutted with impatience. "Well, put it on the table, imbecile!"

"O-of course, Chief Scientist." The befuddled operative placed the pane before Olok and stepped back, face still looking at the metallic floor.

"Switch the thing on -" Olok began but then shook his head and placed a palm on the device. "No, don't trouble yourself. Looks as though I will continue to do everything myself."

The glass rectangle came alive on the table. Images of a fallen hybrid filled the screen.

"As you know, Chief Scientist, drones activate in circumstances where our project subjects have suffered catastrophic damage," the operative said.

Olok held up a spindly arm, forcing the operative to stop talking. "For analysis of flaws in the design and the potential causes of such circumstances. So why have you brought this to me? I have no interest in failed Geno-projects."

The silence rolled out. Olok sighed with irritation. "If you look up from the floor you will see my arm is back on the table and I'm waiting for you to answer the question."

The operative looked up. "Oh, sorry, Chef Scientist! Of course, of course. The interesting data is later, when the drone leaves the cave and records the human."

Olok was suddenly interested. He placed a finger on the right corner of the screen and watched as the footage zipped by until images showed a human and a native species. The human was sitting beside a large male yeti, her hand resting on a mighty forearm. In the background, three other yetis were watching with the same level of curiosity as Olok.

When the human rested a head on the forearm and began to weep, Olok did not see grief.

He saw opportunity.

"Get me an appointment with Administrator Druh. And send out a hunt squad to sector eight," Olok said, standing. "They are not to do anything without direct orders from me, understood?"

"Yes, Chief Scientist."

Olok watched the operative shuffle out. Picking up his vase, he slurped his drink, eyes staring ahead, seeing nothing but salvation.

***

His mind is a reeling, screaming nightmare of grotesque images, a place from which there is no escape. He has been snatched from the life he once knew, the dimension he once belonged, and dropped into hell, where nothing makes sense, and pain is omnipotent.

He tries to hold onto some things, a token attempt to keep his identity. Johns, he remembers his name is Johns, though what this means in the realities of the confusing netherworld he now finds himself is difficult to process. He knows he exists; he knows this is not a dream, and this makes the hideous, pitiful events going on about him even more terrifying.

When he was a man, he was someone who needed stability and control, someone who gave the same edicts to those who employed him.

He recalls the names of those people - Marcus and Grace Appleby, but they are now both dead. Killed by the mountain and betrayal, avalanche, and the mercenaries they attempted to dupe. He witnessed it all, knows it all, even though he was not there all the time. He knows such things because of his present state, his present sense of being. It leaves him connected, to those who are of this world and those who are not, and the dislocation of this existence – of knowing all and understanding little – makes his mind scream.

He feels as though he is not designed to be part of this reality, he is the glue that binds it all, the conduit through which the possible and impossible flows and mixes, like the juices of life and death.

The minds of those who made him this way are equally confused, he has not met their expectations, ceased to become the prize they thought they had procured and nurtured, instead he is a whimsy, something to be studied, something to be explored with sharp hooks that stretch him thin, and mind probes that scratch across his psyche, trying to understand why he does not meet the expectation, trying to understand it so that next time outcomes meet prospects.

He remembers his name is Johns, he remembers what he has lost and knows this place of abstract, dislocating horror is now his world forever. Penalty, perhaps, for his failure to protect those who relied on him so much, or more likely, for disappointing the anticipations of his creators, a scientific flop of significant proportions.

Either way, his screams of despair are the same.

***

Dan waited in the small anteroom; the large door came down as a series of bleeps and clicks ensued. The water that had followed them into the car drained through small grills in the floor, accompanied by a bath-plug gurgle.

He was crouched beside Elspeth who drifted in and out of consciousness. He checked her shoulder where a smile of red, blistered puncture wounds left spots of blood on the surface of her pale skin.

To his right there was a low hum and he found himself standing as another door slipped open, throwing a familiar purple light into the decontamination chamber.

He stepped cautiously out, one foot over the threshold, the other planted firmly in the car. The room was a replica of the one they'd just left behind, same terminals and same recessed panels. Behind him there was a shrill sequence of bleeps that had him turning to locate the origins of the sound.

Elspeth was coming to, as though the trill was reaching into her subconscious like an alarm clock waking her from deep slumber. Dan went back to her and began to carefully drag her out of the decontamination chamber, propping her up against the nearest alloy wall.

The door closed within seconds of them exiting, cutting them off from the recent madness. But the staccato bleeping continued, the sound louder now, and Dan located the source in the pocket of Elspeth's fatigues.

He patted down the pocket panel on her thigh and found the harsh outline of the location tablet which he pulled free. The screen was alive, but the device was in poor shape despite its weatherproofed exterior. The surface was a spiderweb of cracks from an indent at the bottom right of the screen.

"Stewart? Turn the alarm off, baby," Elspeth mumbled and Dan looked down at her puzzled frown.

"Elspeth? It's me, Dan. Are you okay?"

She tried to move and then winced, her left hand going to her right shoulder. "Bastard bit me. What's that noise?"

Dan turned the tablet over in his hands so that she could look at the screen through squinting eyes. "Yeah, the tablet's going apeshit. I think it's busted."

"No, it means the asset is within visual range." She eased herself upright, moaning as she adjusted her beaten body.

"You need to sit still," Dan said.

"I'm okay, I think. I just fainted," she protested but stopped moving all the same. "But I'm not going to lie, that noise is seriously messing with my karma."

"I just need it a little longer," Dan assured her. "Stay here."

"Of that, you can be certain," she said with a weak smile.

Dan held the tablet in one hand, his eyes flitting from the screen to the room ahead. His stomach churned. If the 'assets' were in this room, then the chances of them being behind one of the steel panels was high.

And given the condition of the creatures they'd just seen, his thoughts of locating Appleby at that moment were ambivalent at best.

People on this mission didn't understand him, that much had always been clear. His loyalty towards the Appleby family wasn't exclusive. The seeds had been sown back on The Lion Farm council estate, where Charlie had changed his world for the better. A good boss could do that, inspire through action, true leadership that, over time, Dan had come to worship like a god. Without loyalty how could he hope to have a focus, or purpose for that matter? The cynics in the team would put this down to Grace Appleby, the alluring, brilliant younger wife, a cause for someone like him to blindly follow like a lapdog. But that wasn't who he was, that wasn't why he was here in this room with a bleeping tablet in his palm, and a heavy heart in his chest.

He felt Elspeth's presence beside him. Her curiosity had clearly overridden her discomfort. She was still looking unsteady but was using the terminals and the wall for support, her eyes squinting at the tablet over his shoulder, which had now changed its tone to one continuous burr as they stood before the last terminal in the room.

"We're here," she whispered, taking the tablet from him, and hitting the disconnect switch. The room was startlingly quiet now the location signal was suddenly cut off. She placed the tablet on the terminal without taking her eyes away from the panel.

"Let's get this thing over with," Dan said, his face drawn.

Elspeth manoeuvred herself into the terminal seat and hit the familiar blue button. The screen came to life as the panel hissed open. They both took a moment to comprehend what it was they were looking at before Dan voiced their collective thoughts.

"What the hell is this?"

Elspeth's hand went up to her mouth as they tried to contain the mounting horror as realisation crept into her psyche.

As one, they stared at the thing behind the screen.

***

Mlaa and Mala ran through the rocky passages, their grunts of playful laughter rebounding all about them. As cubs, their ability to play was as much part of their upbringing as learning to hunt and fend for themselves, but the opportunity to do so was a rarity. For so long, Mamma had kept them by her side, keeping them safe from the 'sky people' who sometimes stalked the passageways, or the terrible creatures they created and set free to roam the gloomy tunnels and caverns.

But since the 'human' had shown up, they had sensed a change in their Mamma. It meant that they had, for a second time, been sent off to check out the tunnels and make sure they were free of dangers, and to give the elder-folk time to talk.

The warning from their Mamma had been one of absolute caution, and that had been their intention until, devoid of purpose such as seeking out Lifeblood, their natural, puerile instincts to have fun kicked in. Now, as they charged through the tunnels engaged in a game of tag, the siblings were carefree and young for the first time in an age.

And it was because they were consumed by their newfound freedom, that neither of the cubs saw the alien hunt team lurking further in the tunnel until it was too late. Within a few seconds, mirth and laughter was replaced by the hiss of gas grenades from multiple arc-rifles.

***

Druh adjusted his scatter cushions and leaned back on the generous seating area. His office was a place of opulence, a grandstand for an Administrator of his calibre. He'd been successful for most of his long life, so long and so successful that he had no real idea of how old he was nor how much wealth he'd accrued. Quantum science was a gift and he tended to it well.

His home world was, of course, as distant in lightyears as it was in memory. He had not set foot upon it for hundreds of years, but he visited it often via the psyche tank, attending board meetings regularly, keeping abreast of developments as they occurred in the universe of corporate acquisition.

Druh spooned a mouthful of *spagazzle* into his snout, the tendrils of vegetable matter tickling his pointed chin, covering it with grease. He longed for some authentic, traditional fayre; the synthetic replicators did a good job but there was always something missing from the flavour, something that made it a reminder that it wasn't quite the real thing.

He was resigned to his fate, to administrate a contract of significant worth, with limited margin for error. His assent to this fact led, of course, to Olok; his brilliant - yet maverick - Chief Scientist.

Chewing on his food, Druh considered his own decision to allow humans into the labyrinth. It was true that such an infiltration carried risk, some would suggest such risk was significant, but Druh was a creature who worked on prospective gain. And when dealing with risk, nothing could be considered without, at first, putting in place a means of mitigation.

Especially when it came to his own well-being. There was little doubt that the humans could be irradiated on Druh's orders, the labyrinth had ways of purging them without interference. The swathes of tunnels housed many scientific disasters that would effectively deal with the situation of unwanted trespassers.

But he knew it would be Olok, desperate to complete his project and get off this planet, who would orchestrate such a task. He knew this because he knew his Chief Scientist very well. In telling Olok how things were going to be, Druh had ensured that Olok, motivated by his burgeoning desire to go home, would meddle to keep the project clean and simple, removing any variable that would impede his goal.

And in doing so, give Druh the means needed to dismiss his troublesome employee for insubordination, at least or reckless dereliction of duty if things really went as Druh planned.

Once Olok had delivered on the contract, of course.

Olok was clever but he was also extraordinarily impatient, a trait that the Administrator had never courted. Time was a friend, especially in commerce, getting things right, establishing the protocols to make things effective. Science, he assumed, was the same, an assumption that had held firm until Olok had come onto the project.

The Chief Scientist was well respected in the higher echelons of Balon society, and not an easy employee to manage. His contentious approach had made Olok the perfect fit, but Druh felt his Chief Scientist's arrogance had not taken into account the enormity of the task at hand.

Or the influence of their client.

The Sanctum.

Esoteric and feared, their communication with the outside universe left to trusted intermediaries, fanatical disciples known as *Clerics of Forrestal*, operating out of temples scattered throughout the galaxy. The face of each Cleric was fire-branded with the sigil of the Forrestal Temple, the huge ugly wheals sealing shut their mouths and eyes, their only means of communication were the written word and psychic tele-links.

Druh's mind stalled at the thought of these vile creatures, with their black robes and cowls, and mutilated faces. He'd only met one of their kind once, during the early discussions. That was more than enough for him. The Cleric had oozed malice and contempt for everyone in the boardroom. He remembered thinking that if they could brutalise their own kind, what would they do to outsiders who failed them?

Yet, commerce was always the goal for The Balon Co-operative. Through the Clerics, the contract had been negotiated and refined, line by line and then renegotiated, until signed in secret.

Access to the final agreement was so clandestine, not even Druh had seen the small print. All he had was a list of conditions and, more to his discomfort, the consequences for contractual breach and failure.

He shuddered and put down his fork, his appetite suddenly diminished at the thought of the repercussions of not honouring their agreements. And that was why it was so important to have mitigation in place, contingencies for both success and failure. And, in some ways, Druh was ultimately grateful for the contradictions of his Chief Scientist.

Such things meant that, no matter what the outcome, Druh was destined to remain alive at the end of it all.

"Not a bad outcome," he said to the room. "Not a bad outcome at all."

The notion helped to calm him.

After all, nothing went smoothly all the time, and it was when things didn't go quite according to plan that Druh relished and embraced the challenge. Their latest contract was a difficult proposition but not impossible. Creating living things that are utterly unique took time, but the rewards for meeting the brief were incredible. But it was not about the wealth - though it did soften the blow - it was about the stature that came with success. Renown was his god and, in its temple, he worshipped often and reaped the rewards accordingly.

The intercom sent out a pleasant refrain. "Yes?"

"It's Olok."

There were always irritants, of course. Olok was an exceptional scientist. He was also an annoying fungus that, at in this moment of reflection, Druh could certainly do without.

"What is it, Olok? I'm in the middle of writing board reports." The lie came quick and easily.

"I asked for an audience." Olok's tone was not made any warmer by the lilting intercom.

"This isn't about shooting an operative is it? Because I already know and, frankly, how you manage your junior staff is not a matter for executives."

"I may have found a way forward on our current contract." Olok sounded smug.

Druh tried to hide the intrigue in his voice by speaking through a mouthful of *spagazzle*. "And what is that, Olok?"

"A-way-forward," Olok said pointedly.

Druh clicked his pointed teeth together. "Well, I see you are intent on talking in riddles until I let you up here. Come, you will be on timer."

After disconnecting from the intercom, Druh stood and went to his work desk, a large unwieldly thing made of wood from a planet that no longer existed. Over time, he'd found that war had a habit of making things far more unique. But such practices were limiting in terms of reputation. Anyone could achieve such things through violence, and some of his clients were not proponents of conflict. There was no singular approach in business.

As he sat down behind his desk, the door to his office hissed open and Olok stepped through. The Chief Scientist was animated, moving towards the desk in jaunty steps.

"You have five Earth minutes, Olok. Starting from now." He hit the timer on his desk, the pendulum swinging with a quiet ticking sound.

Olok paced in front of the desk. "We have a contractual obligation to find a creature so unique that our clients have given us unlimited resources, and unlimited time."

Druh watched his Chief Scientist with an impatient air. "Can we move on to a point that I am not already familiar with, Olok?"

Undeterred, Olok continued. "We can only surmise as to why such a creature is so important to them. Frankly, I do not give a Shylock's fin as to why."

Druh drummed his fingers on the desktop. "Please get on with it, Olok. I pay you for science, not drama."

Olok stopped pacing. "We are pioneers on a new frontier. We have to think differently."

"Splicing is what we do. Are you suggesting that you have found an alternative method of organic blending?"

Olok tutted. "No, nothing so simple as that, Druh. We must look beyond the physicality of our task here. Something that connects two species in a manner that goes far beyond the clumsy stitching of flesh or genes. Something that will bind on an intrinsic emotional level. It is *symbolism* that will forge a new era."

"That's impossible," Druh said, though there was no denying the interest in his voice, no matter how much he tried to suppress it.

Olok crossed his thin arms across his chest. "No, that is *unique*. And fulfils our contractual obligations to our clients, yes?"

Druh nodded. "So, what creation could evoke and unite such a response in two different species?"

Olok told him.

Despite his excitement, Druh remained cautious. "And where do you expect to find such a thing? Conjuring is not in our gift."

Olok smiled. "Be at peace, Administrator. The process has already begun."

CHAPTER TWELVE

For the first time in what seems like an age, there is clarity in the void. Something is coming to him through the maelstrom, thoughts of others, other people. He connects, relishing the warmth of human contact, an association he never thought he would miss. But miss it he does, because he is human, despite the hooks and the scratches of the mind probes, he is part of a great race of people, flawed to be sure, but united in their belief of hope and love, constructs that now, in this raw and vulnerable state, are almost overpowering in their scope, threatening to crush him under the weight of the mountain, and this metaphor makes his mind laugh because he is already physically as flat as a fluke worm, a pliable, malleable flap of skin, devoid of form.

He can connect but he cannot influence, he needs to be invited, asked to meld with the minds of those coming to him. He will barter, he will give them what they need in return for what he desires more than anything in this depraved new world.

Death.

Sweet nothingness, devoid of pain and misery, without the terrible burdens he carries on behalf of everyone who has wronged and destroyed in the name of science and profit.

Not long now, he can feel his excitement rising like a leviathan from the depths, a surge of hope that he will achieve the nothingness he now craves. He also feels something else, intruders that push against the psychic shield he has forged around himself, the protection for his sanity. Others are interested in his connection with those nearby, those who see, not failure, but cosmic opportunity for this experiment to continue, for his torment to play out in the name of theological discovery.

Frustrated, he closes off the connection, but the primary issue is to thwart the understanding of those attempting to gate-crash any attempt to communicate, to add distraction to his purpose.

He will bide his time, and when the moment comes, his revelations will be brief and damning.

And his quest for release, achieved.

***

Vision fogged by the effects of alien stun-gas, Mlaa lay on her back, struggling to make sense of what was going on. She could feel rock beneath her, and there was a vague shape lying prone nearby. She reached out, feeling the coarse fur of her brother.

"Mala!" Her grunts were thick, vocal cords still reluctant to work after their chemical emasculation.

Mala stirred, giving out a protracted groan. Relieved, Mlaa sat up, her vision beginning to clear. Although her body was heavy with fatigue, and her head throbbed, the dull, approaching footfalls forced her to focus on what was going on about them.

She used her fingers to wipe away grit and sticky mucus coating her eyelids. Then she saw the many alien troopers, weapons poised in their direction.

A voice came from nearby. "Are you afraid?"

"Do not hurt us," she whispered.

"I asked are you afraid?"

Head bowed, Mlaa said, "Yes, I am afraid."

"Then you must do what all children do when they are afraid."

Olok stepped from the rank of guards and peered down at her. "You must call out for your mother."

***

Inside the containment chamber, Elspeth and Dan looked on, aghast.

Behind the glass, there was no ocean or jungle landscape, there was only a room with metal walls, illuminated in harsh white light. At the centre stood an upright, rectangular frame, the outline made from thick, alloy beams, with blinking lights and buttons embedded into the structure.

There was something spread-eagled inside the frame. Hooks had been strategically placed, piercing the skin, then attached to taut wires that were retracted into the edifice, stretching the skin until what remained was a grey, jagged silhouette.

It had once been a man, the outline was clear on that, but there was no longer substance, and the face was pulled into a grotesque screaming mask, eyes gone, manhood a flaccid condom of flesh left to sway, a thing that should not exist, let alone live.

Because live it still did, both Elspeth and Dan could see the wretched apparition shudder in its frame like a sail on the sea breeze.

"That's not Appleby," Dan said. Elspeth noted that he sounded relieved.

"It's Johns." Her voice came as a whisper.

Dan was aghast. "What have they done to him?"

Elspeth looked down at the monitor on her workstation. Once more, Johns was on display, this time as a one-dimensional picture, no rotation, and glowing from the computer model, a series of irradiated clouds billowed, making the image eerily beautiful.

"He's giving out an aura," Elspeth said.

"This is a fucking freak show." Dan's voice was breaking.

As Dan spoke, Elspeth saw the aura about Johns' image change to reds and oranges on the screen.

"He can hear us," she said.

"What? How do you know that?"

"The aura, it changed when you spoke. Somehow he can hear what we're saying."

"Through reinforced glass?"

Elspeth's voice was low with a terrible awe. "The poor guy shouldn't be alive, but he is. And those creatures managed to break through the glass. Maybe they've all got the same thing in common, they're determined enough to be free."

Dan nodded and faced the panel. "Johns, can you hear me?"

"Yes. Kill me. Please. Kill me."

Surprised, Dan's mouth fell open. Not because he'd had a response, nor that Johns' statement was as pitiful as it was astounding to hear. No, the reason that Dan was stunned was that the words were not spoken by Johns at all.

They came from Elspeth.

***

Knowles woke with a start. She'd been dreaming of spiders and yetis and endless tunnels lit with silvery, cream light. When she looked about her, her heart sank to see that, these days, dreams were very much a reality.

She'd fallen asleep on the chair next to the table where Sully now lay peacefully, his great chest rising and falling, and great snorts powering out of his nostrils.

"How the hell I managed to sleep through that chain-saw is anybody's guess," Knowles mused. She looked about her, finding the dwelling now empty. The firepit was now smouldering, having served its purpose.

Knowles had eaten the food prepared by Maal, a mixture of dried meats, berries and herbs in a broth made from hot spring water the cubs had brought back after another expedition into the tunnel system. The broth didn't taste good and it didn't taste bad, it merely filled her belly, pushing away the gnawing hunger that had settled into her gut as soon as she smelled the first aroma of cooking.

Sully had woken briefly to take on board some sustenance but fell asleep again soon after. He'd lost a lot of blood and, under normal circumstances, would take some time to recover. But as she knew, things were far from normal. The Lifeblood was working its alien magic on his body, sealing his wound, repairing tissue, reinvigorating the physiological systems that kept her friend as formidable as ever.

Before Knowles had dozed off, the firepit had been ablaze, now she could see that time had passed, an hour, maybe two, where she'd succumbed to her fatigue. She recalled talking to Maal for some time after their meal, hearing about some of her travels through the subterranean world, giving Knowles a fascinating insight as to how the small family had managed to survive beneath the mountain. The important thing, Maal had told her, was that family meant everything, and without them Maal could not go on.

Knowles understood this but hearing it from such a resolute fighter like Maal was a surprise. It certainly reinforced Knowles' belief that they were doing the right thing, to avenge those who were lost to the alien invaders.

Standing up, Knowles went to the doorway as Sully's snoring stopped and he snorted once before sitting up, the table beneath him creaking, threatening to give way and dump him onto the floor.

"Hey, take it easy, big fella," Knowles said, coming over to him. "You've had a busy day."

"Sully feels better," he said, voice thick from sleep.

"Well, Sully needs to take it easy otherwise that table is going to collapse."

Rising from the table, he stood, wavered for a moment, and shook his head furiously.

"What the hell are you doing?" Knowles said in panic.

"Time to wake up."

"You're likely to put yourself back into a coma."

Ignoring her, he went on to stretch out his limbs, grunting with the effort. His right thigh had healed, leaving a mere puckered scar, the fur about it gone.

"Bald leg," he said as he examined the scar.

"Yeah," Knowles said sadly. "You were lucky, fella. Maal and her cubs did good."

Sully looked about the dwelling. "Gone?"

"Observant. Not sure where."

It occurred to Knowles that, perhaps, Maal and her cubs had decided to move on. It was their way of dealing with things, after all. The thought left her feeling a little dejected. While in her company, Knowles had garnered insights into the importance of family and, dare she say it, some hope for the trials to come.

Her wistful thoughts were unexpectedly broken when a great roar filled the cavern, not of anger but of despair.

Knowles and Sully rushed outside, and there they saw Maal stumbling across the chamber. She was pointing behind her, towards the Elder's dwelling.

Knowles went to her. "What is it?"

"Cubs hurt. Trapped." Maal was panting with exertion and panic.

"Where?" Sully growled.

"In cave of beast."

Knowles tried to make sense of Maal's words. Then she remembered the hybrid and the hole it had made in the wall of the Elder's sleeping area.

"The cubs went into the wall?" Knowles said in horror.

Maal nodded frantically. "Young and foolish. Now they call to me, they are trapped, hurt."

"We have to go to them. Help them out." Knowles headed off, but Sully held back.

"Maal is Mamma. Responsible for her cubs."

"Sully, are you joking? She saved your hairy ass."

To Knowles' despair, she saw Maal nod an accord. "Sully is right. Not your duty."

"To hell with that," Knowles said angrily. She turned to Sully. "We're all in this shit together, Sully. Those things are at war with us all, you get that?"

"We have our ways," Sully said, looking at the ground and scuffing the grit with his foot.

"I get that," Knowles said softly. "But if you want to have any chance of keeping traditions, you have to be *alive*. And these bastards want to kill us all. We have to look out for each other."

Sully's big brown eyes scrutinised Knowles for so long she thought he'd gone into a trance. Then he looked away and towards the Elder's dwelling.

"Okay," he said and marched off. Shaking her head in confusion, Knowles watched him go.

"Fucker's almost as stubborn as I am," she said to herself, smiling.

***

Elspeth blinked, sure her eyes were playing tricks on her, or that the bite from the amphibious creature was venomous, and alien toxins were now going to town on her central nervous system. She questioned these things because at that moment she was sitting in her favourite eatery, *Caffe Concerto* in London's West End, flat white and a tuna melt on the table in front of her.

Sitting opposite was a man. From the file she'd read prior to leaving Pokhara, she knew he was Johns, the chief security advisor for Professor Marcus Appleby. His image in the file was out of date, but certainly more flattering than the stretched skinsuit she'd seen only moments before.

"Why are you in my head?" she said. Her fingers toyed with the edges of her sandwich. It smelled so good her stomach growled.

He paused for a few moments, collecting his thoughts. "Crimes have been committed here. Heinous crimes, against so many living things. They need to be punished."

"You can't be here," she said, rubbing her brow as if to be free of him. "You *shouldn't* be here."

Johns agreed with a nod. "I know. I'm trespassing. In most parts of the universe such an event is also crime. But we're so far away from such worlds. We're playing catch up."

"But what can we do?" she said.

"Stay alive."

"That's proving easier said than done." She'd meant it as a thought but realised there were no secrets in this place.

Johns leaned in. "I can help you. Keep you safe."

"Why would you do that?"

His reply was ferociously blunt. "Because I ask for mercy. I'm in great pain and I want it to end."

"What happened to you, to the Applebys?"

Johns told her.

She bowed her head. "So, we risked our lives for nothing."

"Not nothing. You can save me. And in return I can show you the means to save the universe."

She looked up so fast she felt her neck creak. "The universe?"

Johns closed his eyes, his face creased as though recalling terrible things. "I've reached out across the cosmos, touched the void between worlds. I have been cursed with knowledge that I should not have but we are blessed with a warning."

"Of what?"

He opened his eyes, they were haunted. "The trials to come."

"For us?"

"For us. For all living things."

"I'm not sure I understand."

Her confession earned her a nod of appreciation from the man across the table. "You will. In time you will. But you must survive. And I must die."

She frowned. "You want us to kill you. How can you help us if we do as you ask?"

Johns gestured to the cafe. "Allow us this place. A memory sectioned away in the recess of your mind. Keep me here, in the calm."

"You mean give you a part of my mind?" Her face betrayed the horror she felt at such a notion.

"No. I mean I will give you part of mine. And with it will come knowledge of the greatest secrets of the cosmos, the greatest threat, a chance to stop it from happening at all."

Elspeth could sense panic rising within her. "But I don't want this knowledge."

"You don't want the *responsibility*. I understand your worry. But not knowing does not stop what will happen if we don't act."

"I don't trust you." There, now it was out and wanton.

But Johns merely smiled as though this was the most obvious response in the world. "How can you trust me if you don't trust yourself? You still can't forgive yourself for something that happened so long ago."

"I'm uncomfortable with that topic." Her eyes glazed, becoming cold.

Johns held up his hands. "Sorry, out of bounds, I get it. Your punishment is as painful as mine. But we can come here, our own mutual sanctuary. The only place I can be at a time of only your choosing. One-way traffic."

"Shit," she muttered.

Her choices were limited right now. Without help it was only a matter of time before their luck ran out and their incredible enemies caught up with them. A shudder ran through her when she thought of what had happened to Johns and the other creatures who had found themselves at the mercy of the invaders. As deals went, this was the only fucking thing on the table.

"Okay," she said. "Okay, we have an agreement. But first there must be rules. My mind, my rules - you get me?"

"Of course."

"No taking over, no prying, no doing anything fucking *weird*."

Johns laughed and it was a pleasant sound. "I'm not a ghost, Elspeth. You're not going to need an exorcism after we strike a deal. I will be inert unless you ask something of me."

She sat back, thoughtful. "I can't believe I'm doing this," she sighed. "Okay, I agree to it. But only because I have no real choice. So how do we do this?"

"You just have to think it. Free will is a powerful thing."

A waitress came over and stood next to Johns. "What can I get for you, sir?"

Johns smiled and gave his order. The waitress made a note and pushed her pencil behind her ear before walking away.

"Thank you," he said.

He was looking at Elspeth.

CHAPTER THIRTEEN

The hole in the wall had them all pausing on the threshold. It was a daunting image, a black teardrop where something both hideous and miserable had emerged to do great harm to them all.

On the way through the dwelling, Sully had retrieved his great club, and had it slung across his right shoulder as he took in the surroundings. Behind them, the fallen hybrid was now a mouldering husk. Unseen cave creatures had gone to work on it in the time they'd been away, and all flesh from the yeti had been stripped and shredded and pieces lay scattered across the rugged floor.

Knowles had spent a few moments going over the corpse and noted that there was a seam of pure silver joining the yeti and the spider, and from this seam what she thought at first to be tendrils wove their way up the skeleton's spine. On closer examination, she saw that these were not tendrils but wires and piping, alien tech designed to fuse two species together in unholy alliance.

"Motherfuckers," she'd whispered but Sully overheard her and placed a big, comforting hand on her shoulder. She patted it by way of thanks.

"Let's try and make this right for Maal," she said, and he nodded his great head.

Sully had to give Maal reassurance to stop her from charging into the cave to rescue her cubs. He placed his forehead to hers in a clear gesture of comfort and this took the heat out of her rage. After a few minutes they entered, Sully leading the way, his club ready to deliver a powerful blow should something come at them.

Initially the darkness was daunting, and they each placed a hand on the other so that no one would be lost to the void. But, after a few metres, the tunnel veered left, and Knowles began to see shapes as the quality of light improved.

Soon enough, as they went further, the familiar creamy light was bathing the rocks and allowed them to follow the path that took them on a downward trajectory. Knowles was able to make out deep scratches in the dirt where the hybrid had marked its passage through the tunnels. She shivered at the thought of what might have been had the creature succeeded.

This had her thinking about the alien's endgame. From what she'd seen of them so far, their methods indicated more science than soldiering, a terrible science admittedly but there was no denying this was their preferred mandate. This inevitably led her to thinking about existence under the yoke of these beings, the terrible possibilities that may befall life on Earth, with all living things becoming slaves to a grand science experiment in an alien lab. She found the anger this evoked embittered her thinking and she closed it down.

Deeper into the tunnels, the walls seemed to morph into giant boulders, fused together into great shapes that looked to Knowles unsettlingly like behemoths frozen in slumber. The light also appeared to be changing, the creamy hue was starting to adopt a purple tinge, and Knowles had the feeling she'd seen this kind of thing before, the precursor to caves and caverns becoming under the influence of alien technology.

"Where were the twins when you last saw them?" Knowles said to Maal as the tunnels opened out into a large chamber.

"Other side of cavern. In the purple light."

"Purple light bad," Sully pointed out.

"Yeah, okay, big fella, Now's not the time to bring a downer on events."

They kept to the periphery, making sure there were enough rock structures between them and the open ground ahead. Across the void, Knowles took in the incredible sight of a sphere with multiple tendrils. When she saw the line of aliens, a countless number, all armed with arc-rifles, she realised it was a spacecraft.

But at the entrance, there were two figures incongruent to those about them, Mala and Mlaa. The cubs were huddled up together in fear, a squad of alien troopers aiming arc-weapons at their shivering forms. They began calling out for their mamma, fear and anguish in their voices breaking Knowles' heart.

"Those fuckers are so dead," she growled.

Maal was suddenly barging past, despite the hissed calls from Knowles. The yeti broke cover and headed straight for the alien troopers who watched her come with indifference.

"There's something wrong," Knowles said as shadows fell upon both her and Sully. They looked up and, scurrying along a rocky ridge, several aliens had weapons trained upon them. Footfalls from the tunnel behind told Knowles that they were surrounded.

Sully tensed, his hand on the club gripping so tightly, Knowles could hear the joints of his fingers popping. She placed a hand on his forearm.

"No. They'll kill you."

"Listen to your companion. It will save your life."

The voice came from the clearing. Knowles turned to see a squad of alien warriors led by a smaller figure, thin body shrouded in a flowing grey robe, the material crackling as it walked. With the entourage came Maal, her head lowered in shame, the cubs clutching her waist, terrified.

Keeping her head down, Maal addressed Knowles and Sully in a small desperate voice. "Forgive, Maal. Sky people say they kill cubs if I not bring you here."

Knowles understood. And she hated seeing this once proud creature reduced to treachery in order to survive. She glared instead at the alien figure who was examining his fingers in apparent tedium.

"You bastards are going to pay for everything you've done on this planet," Knowles seethed.

Olok stopped his preening. "Very noble. Misguided, ill-informed and statistically impossible, but yes, very noble indeed."

He stepped forwards, without fear or trepidation, and addressed Sully, who held his club as though he was waiting to hit a home run.

"I very much hope that you drop that lump of rock without the need for violence."

"Do it, Sully," Knowles said without taking her eyes from Olok. "This asshole isn't worth it."

"We all have our worth," Olok said, his voice rising and falling as though he was trying out its range. "But there is a time limit. And, sadly, for some, that limit is at an end."

Without warning, and to the abject disbelief of both Knowles and Sully, the troopers stepped away from Maal and her cubs. As the troopers lifted their weapons, the female yeti let out a strangled roar, the product of rage and terror. She grabbed the nearest alien warrior and broke him in two across her knee; the cubs savaged another, its blood splattering their fur.

The defence was admirable but, as Olok had already prophesised, ultimately futile. The arc-rifles spoke, too many to count, tearing into the three yetis, charring fur, and flesh, the results effective and merciless.

Knowles found the cries of pain and distress almost too much to bear. Tears coursed down her cheeks, blurring the terrible image of murder but not erasing it in her mind.

Sully's mighty, savage roar echoed about the chamber. He lifted the club despite Knowles' cry to desist and jumped into the clearing. He smashed two aliens aside with a blow from the club, their shattered bodies flapping through the air like birds shot from the sky.

Knowles ran to him, desperate to reason with him, to protect him, but there was an explosion of green mist that obscured the scene. Knowles and Sully found themselves struggling for breath, their minds as fogged as the hideous event in front of them.

Knowles scrambled to Sully, who placed an arm about her, keeping her close.

It was to be the last thing that either of them would remember until they came around in Olok's lab sometime later.

***

The elevator doors opened, and Bart limped out onto a gangway. The wind howled about him, whipping at his clothing, snatching away his breath. It was mere moments before he understood he was someplace high in the cave system's infrastructure, and as he limped onto a causeway of mesh alloy, and peered over the edge, he was dumbstruck at just how lofty his vantage point was in comparison to where he'd started out.

The walls were several feet away, and were made of pure metal, their corrugated surfaces creating vertical stripes of light and shadow under the spotlights secured to the concourse, the slashes getting smaller the further away they became, creating a confounding sense of perspective.

Bart checked out the area about him, where the gangway seemed to link with a series of circular platforms, forming a matrix of walkways and small booths. The nearest booth was not distant, a mere thirty metres from his current point. Feeling exposed, the decision to make for the stall as cover seemed a sensible one, and he made his way towards it with a cautious urgency.

As he moved, Bart thought of what was going on with the others, whether they had met the same fate as he and Collins, ambushed on the mountain by those incredible machines, or succumbing to the hideous creature lurking in the mountain.

Bart didn't know much of Dan; they had only been introduced shortly before leaving Pokhara's small airport in Collins' chopper. Dan hadn't really communicated much but Bart didn't take that to heart as he'd noted that the man had been just as surly with everyone.

Elspeth and Chris he'd known for a lot longer, several years, in fact. They had been on a few geographical expeditions together, once in Colombia; Bart to undertake the topographical surveys, Elspeth to monitor local traffic and infrastructure of local law enforcement, and Chris as leader of the ten-strong security team protecting them all. But their relationship was based on professional respect and their excursions were for commercial research and investment opportunities, not associated with rescue missions in any shape or form. He figured that Dan was probably not quite as inexperienced and secretly hoped that it would be this that kept Elspeth and Chris safe.

If they were all still alive of course.

Bart shut down these thoughts before they could impede his ability to act. He continued his journey down the causeway, the cone-shaped booth becoming ever closer. As he navigated his way through the egress from concourse to platform, Bart made sure he was still alone. The platform was hexagonal and serviced at each axis by a similar gangway to the one he had just left behind. He assumed that these new walkways led to elevators or even other buildings, and when he thought of the intricacies of this network, so it was that his mind became awed by the implications for the mountain.

What was becoming apparent to him was that the creatures who had ensnared them on the mountain were far from isolated and he began to fear their numbers. The important thing for him now, however, was to find a craft to get him out of here to get help for the others. But there was no sign of any form of transport from what he could see at that moment.

He reached the booth and sought out access. There was no recognisable handle visible, but there was a silver stud with a winking red light. Bart placed his thumb on the stud and a section of wall depressed then slipped to one side.

He was walking into the booth when he heard a bleeping coming from far off. It was brought to him on the wind that slapped into his face, betraying the direction from which the sound had come.

The beep was familiar, another elevator had docked, somewhere on the other end of a concourse. Soon it would be allowing whoever had just arrived to disembark, and sure enough, he heard the distant clatter of feet – many feet – hitting the causeway.

Ducking inside, he tried to find the means to shut the door but was out of luck. He moved further into the booth, hoping the low lighting would shield him from whoever was walking up one of the gangways. However, the overhead lights clicked on, Bart falling foul of an alien motion-activated system.

The cubicle was oval, a run of shelves following the curved walls. On the shelves were boxes that housed many items that Bart didn't recognise. But he did notice the spools of wire and piping, and some metal tubes with sprockets that made him conclude this was a maintenance room for servicing the elevators.

Underneath each shelf were metal gurneys, and Bart slid one free. Here he found containers stacked in rows of three across two shelves, their cylindrical surfaces smooth and black with a series of coiled pipes leading to a short lance, ending in a nozzle.

"Welding kit?" he surmised.

The footfalls outside were getting louder. He tried to quell the panic rising in his chest. This wasn't what he needed right now. He needed time to think things through, to be scientific – clinical – about a way to get through this mess.

All he had to defend himself with was a knife and some wire. And he was inside a confined space with a light that may as well have said "here he is, suck his brains out".

But something dropped into his head. A deduction, scientific reasoning coming to his aid when he needed it the most. Before he could talk himself out of what some would consider an act of scientific recklessness, Bart acted.

He navigated the gurney into the doorway and charged, despite the protest from his aching ankle, setting the course for the causeway where a line of alien creatures was making their way towards the platform. Bart struggled to maintain focus when he saw the images of misshapen heads with large fisheyes and grey snouts moving in unison, but his incredulity was countered by scientific reality.

This was reinforced seconds later when a bolt of rheumy light snaked across the platform and a shower of sparks hit a handrail behind him. Motivated by a burning need to stay alive, Bart pushed the gurney with all his might, letting go when he'd reached his optimum velocity, the trajectory now taking the welding equipment and fuel cells towards the egress at the end of the causeway.

The light from the booth winked out, its timer now spent. Several arc-rifles sent bolts into the structure, riddling it with explosions, the glass shattering, the exterior heaving under the onslaught.

This distraction was enough for Bart to climb to his feet and try to put distance between him and the inevitable. With a crash, the gurney struck the egress, an instinctive arc-rifle blast followed a second later. Then the platform was a place of brilliant white light.

The next thing Bart realised was that his world was on fire.

***

Dan dropped to his knees and scanned Elspeth's face, troubled that her eyes were wide but glazed, as though she was looking straight through him. It was an unnerving sensation, taking him back to a time when his grandmother had been in hospital, trying to fight off pneumonia.

He'd been eight at the time, his gran in her sixties, young by today's standards. But the illness was working hard on her lungs and a lifetime of smoking didn't help her respiratory issues. As she lay in the bed, the air smelling of disinfectant and bad breath, his grandmother's lips had been moving silently, and he'd leaned in to stand a better chance of catching what she was saying. When he sat back up again, there was the glazed stare, only this time his gran's mouth had gone slack, like invisible wires were stitched to the corners of her mouth, pulling downwards. She had died several minutes later.

He shrugged off the memory. "Elspeth? Are you okay?"

To his relief she blinked and shook her head slightly. At first, he thought she was responding to his question, then he realised she was shaking herself awake.

He waved a hand in front of her. "Hey, you with me?"

"Yes." She stood up, her gait shaky, and she used the workstation to stabilise herself as she adjusted. "We have to go."

Caught out, Dan remained on his knees before he realised what was happening. "Yeah, I get that but let's get a handle on what just happened, okay?"

"Johns is dead. The Applebys are dead. And we must get out of here, now."

He jumped up. "Wait! What do you mean 'the Applebys are dead'? How do you know that for sure?"

Elspeth seemed relax, her shoulders sagging a little. "Take a look at Johns."

"What?"

"Just do it," she urged. "Take a look at him and tell me what you see."

With hesitance, Dan went back to the viewing panel and looking inside. Johns was no longer taut on the frame, the lines had unwound, and like discarded laundry, his skin lay as a heap of folds on the ground. The machines keeping him in such a state were now giving out smoke, turning the room behind the glass to a haze.

"What happened to him?" Dan said, his head turning and resting on the panel.

Elspeth tapped a finger against her temple. "He's in here."

Dan's face caught up with her words a few seconds later. "Are you on substances or something? Why would you do that?"

Elspeth stood upright, defiant. "He knows how we can get out of here. I said we'd help him if he helped us."

"Jesus, Elspeth! He could be telling us anything. Leading us into a trap," Dan said in exasperation.

Sighing, Elspeth went to the corner of the room, and placed a palm on an area of wall. There was a small click and a drawer slipped open. She reached inside and pulled out two silver orbs, both with a handle and a muzzle. She offered one to Dan.

"See? Weapons," she said.

He took the gun, feeling its weight. It didn't really have any, like a cheap toy from *Poundland*.

She continued. "Why would someone who didn't want to help us give us the means to defend ourselves?"

Dan appeared as though he could think of many reasons but decided instead to not challenge her. "What happened to Marcus and Grace?"

Elspeth's tone was flat, matter of fact. "They hired mercenaries called The Sebs to come to the mountain, the mission was need-to-know, Johns doesn't have all the details. The team's camp was attacked, and Johns was snatched by what everyone thought was a yeti. Turns out it was one of those alien things we saw topside. He was saved by The Sebs, but not before he was stung by something placed there by the aliens. Whatever it was did *that* to him. There was a plane, it was carrying illicit diamonds, and Marcus and Grace were trying to recover them. They planned to execute the remaining mercenaries and came off second best in the firefight."

"I don't believe it," Dan said but Elspeth saw by the look on his face that he did. Every damn word because it made total sense. Here, in this crazy upside-down world, nothing could have been clearer.

Elspeth stepped up to him and placed a hand on his arm. "They're gone, Dan. Johns saw it all. We're chasing ghosts. I'm sorry."

Dan nodded, face grim, and for a second Elspeth thought she saw his eyes mist over.

He turned away before she could be sure. "So, where we going?"

Elspeth pondered on this, eyes closed. Then, she was back. "We have to find someone. Johns says she's the way out of all this."

"She?"

"He says her name is Clarice Knowles, one of the surviving members of The Sebs."

He was cautious. "One of the people who killed Marcus and Grace?"

"That fight is done," she said flatly. "This is about something much bigger. And Clarice is key to it all."

"What? You mean she can get us out of here?"

"She can save the future."

"I don't know what that means but I'm fucking done trying to understand it." He re-examined the pistol, his brain making sense of its mechanism. "I guess we're moving forwards?"

She nodded. There was a faint smile on her lips as though she knew something he didn't, and it did not sit well with him.

"You got something else to say?" he snapped but she shook her head.

"No. But Johns has plenty. Let's go."

CHAPTER FOURTEEN

On her twenty-first birthday, Knowles had been stationed in Cyprus. Her platoon operated out of Akrotiri base on the southernmost tip of the island and was on a two-day period of leave. To celebrate Knowles' special occasion, they went on a one-day bender involving Leon beer, Zivania spirits and Cypriot Brandy Sours. The events of the time were a blur; most of it, mercifully, forgotten.

When it came, the hangover had been beyond spectacular. The following day seemed to be a period of drifting in and out of consciousness with warped images of her platoon looming over her, a mix of gleeful and concerned faces. Oh, and vomiting, so much in fact she tore muscles in her diaphragm, making her think that she was suffocating. Then came the embarrassment of waking up in the field hospital, on a drip for dehydration and a misconduct charge sitting in the wings.

Since that event, Knowles had not touched a drop of alcohol, but the recovery experience had cemented itself in her brain, a warning to keep her on the straight and narrow.

Yet the vile sensation she'd experienced when recovering from alcohol poisoning was what she found as she returned to consciousness. She'd also had images pass through her mind, but rather than her platoon, these were of hideous things with fisheyes and grey skin, wearing surgical gowns and masks, and long slender fingers holding silver implements.

She groaned, her hands going to her head which felt as though it wanted to explode. Her stomach did a roll and she gagged. In an instant, she felt the sting of a needle in her thigh and the nausea and headache disappeared after a few seconds, clearing her faculties, and allowing her to open her eyes.

The room about her was akin to that of a hospital Intensive Care Unit, but the machinery and furnishings were off kilter, their structures ovoid and consisting of shimmering metal. There were no readouts or 'pinging' noises, and the few wires on show were plugged into her arm.

Sully was also there, lying on a gurney, thick bands of light wrapped about his arms and chest, thighs, and ankles, pinning him in place.

Like an angry bee, a silver orb buzzed about the bed, twin tendrils hanging from its body, and a tiny hypodermic needle was held fast in its small slender fingers. Knowles recalled the recent sting in her thigh and realised this was her saviour from the pseudo-hangover.

The disorientation waning, she sat up. The orb retreated to the wall on the left, where it landed on a white shelf and, after a series of clicks, lay silent.

On the opposite side of the room, a rectangle of glass reflected her own image. She knew the score; there was going to be something behind that screen, staring at her and Sully, scrutinising.

Swinging her legs from the gurney, she planted her bare feet on the floor, suddenly aware of the short, silver surgical gown she was wearing. An unsettling feeling of exposure came over her; those things had undressed her and manipulated her when she was at her most vulnerable.

At the same moment as she recognised her raiment, she became aware of a dull ache in her lower abdomen, and her hands went to the site, probing it with her fingers. There was no real discomfort, she merely felt bruised, yet on the insides.

A low growl came to her and she looked over at Sully who was slowly coming to, his great head rolling to one side to look at her. His eyes were slightly glazed as though his brain hadn't quite decided if it liked the idea of waking up or not.

She went over to him, her hands reaching out for the iridescent straps.

"I would advise against making contact with the restrictors." The voice came from overhead, startling Knowles enough to have her step back from her friend.

She turned to the rectangle of glass. "Where the fuck are you?"

Without warning, the reflective pane turned opaque and Olok stood watching her, two associates flanked him, writing notes on their flat, handheld devices.

"There, hope this makes our conversation a little more congenial." Olok's harsh voice sounded anything but cordial.

Knowles removed any doubt in her mood. "Fuck you."

"What is this word 'fuck'?" Olok said to one of his associates. After a brief examination of the device in his hand, the tech showed the screen to Olok. There was an odd sound and Knowles realised it was laughter. "How apt."

Knowles didn't like the way he said these words but held fire. "What are you doing on our planet?"

"Believe me when I say, I have no desire to be here."

Knowles just glared at him.

Olok opened his arms wide as if embracing her question for the first time. "Like you, we are explorers, we are in search of impossible things."

"You're not like us," Knowles replied, her voice bitter.

Olok shook his head, appearing genuinely confused. "Are you not on this mountain for personal gain? A soldier under contract?"

"That's not the same thing." She shuffled on the spot, suddenly uncomfortable with her own answer.

"We provide services that may be considered nefarious by some. Is it any less noble a cause as that provided by you and your 'Sebs'?" Olok said.

Knowles' stare was cool. "Don't mention that term. You're not fit to say it."

Olok shook his head. "Mercenaries. The suggestion you are anything more is contractual delusion. I find this hypocrisy far more offensive than you do my utterance of a namesake."

"You really don't. We've not bastardised races for our own amusement." Knowles' tone was razor-sharp. "Nor murdered innocent mothers and their children."

"The yeti female and her cubs betrayed you. Disloyalty is a heinous crime; the punishment was proportionate. They were executed, not murdered. And you misunderstand the purpose behind the hybrids. They are how we can meet our obligations to our employer. It is not barbarity, it is commerce."

"Dress it up however you want. I don't give a shit. You're invading our world and that makes you my enemy."

Olok seemed genuinely puzzled. "This is no invasion. Such things are not our concern. This planet is off the charts, insignificant, if you will. You have resources available in most civilised galaxies. Nothing special at all, I'm afraid."

"What of those war machines? Thousands of them in the base we destroyed," Knowles said.

He chuckled. "Again, you seem to be drawing wrong conclusions based on a flawed hypothesis. Those machines were for another contract, another employer. War is business, you and your kind should understand that more than most. Fortunately, we were well ahead of schedule on this contract so will not breach terms by missing the deadline. Personally, I think as machines of war, the design is completely useless. But I'm a scientist. What do I know of such matters?"

"I want out of this place." There was only hate in Knowles' words. It oozed from each syllable.

Olok scratched at the side of his head. "Well, this is where we start having a problem."

"You seriously think I'm just going to stand here and let you guys come in without a fight?"

"I would expect you to attempt self-preservation. Alas, you are now part of our contractual obligation. You are the reason why our hybrid programme is now shelved. You have achieved your aim, preserved your kind. What happens next is in your hands, Clarice Knowles."

Knowles was startled by Olok's use of her full name. "How'd you know that?"

"Brain scans show all. Such a rebellious nature," Olok chided.

"You don't know half of it."

"But I do, and I know what you are capable of, including your recklessness. I am here to offer you terms. If you will hear them?"

The seconds ticked out. She finally yielded to buy some more. "Go on."

"You acquiesce and leave with us." Olok regarded her with lifeless eyes.

Knowles laughed. "No way."

"Your planet will be free of us. You get to be the unsung hero, saviour of your world."

"What about Sully?"

"He comes too. That is quite important."

"Why?"

Olok's voice adopted a softer edge. "Because you care about each other very much. And therefore, it is the component that will make this experiment viable."

"What are you talking about? Experiment, what experiment?"

"You may want to sit down, Clarice."

"It's Knowles."

Olok paused, then continued. "Still, I would sit down. This may come as a surprise."

"I'll stand."

"You are with child," Olok said bluntly.

Knowles' legs gave out and she sat down.

**

Dan examined the door at the end of the viewing room. His mood was still bitter, the news of Marcus and Grace Appleby's demise was a body-blow to him. Although it was impossible, Dan felt he was somehow responsible. The notion of guilt was a throwback to his upbringing and the way he dealt with emotional pain ever since the death of his sister. Charlie had tried to give him insight and Dan had eventually accepted it as part of his personality.

He didn't, however, like it.

And the thought that one of the very people who had brought about the demise of Marcus and Grace Appleby was now off the hook because of some higher purpose was equally riling. He wasn't quite sure if he could trust himself not to get even if they actually caught up with Clarice Knowles, or whoever the hell she was.

"You okay?"

Elspeth caught him off-guard and he flinched a little. "Yeah. How's your shoulder?"

She made circular motions with her right arm. "Seems Johns has fixed it."

"Crazy days," he muttered.

His fingers went to the control panel and he punched the keypad. A red warning light flickered, the whole panel becoming crimson.

"Seems it's been overridden," he observed.

"Failsafe. Because of the breach next door," Elspeth said with confidence.

He nodded. "Johns is a bit of a know-all, right?"

Smiling, Elspeth peered upwards. There was nothing by way of egress, just a row of strip lights with their ominous purple hue. Then she looked at the floor and saw the grills. She squatted, curling her fingers into the lattice pattern, and pulled. The grill came away with ease to reveal a deep gully.

She grinned up at him. "Ventilation canal. No overspill from next door."

Dan investigated the ditch. "Must be self-sealing, like a bulkhead on a ship."

Elspeth dropped into the space which came up to her waist. She went to her knees, then to her belly, crawling forwards, the pistol held out before her.

"You coming or not?" she grunted.

Dan watched her shuffle out of sight, creating room for him, and he joined her moments later.

"Where the hell are we headed?" he griped. "It's too cramped to defend ourselves in here. If it all goes off, chances are high I'm going to end up shooting you in the arse with a ray gun."

"I'm guessing you never thought that was a sentence you'd ever get to say in your lifetime."

They both chuckled, moving onwards, the gully thankfully widening after twenty metres as it sloped downwards, opening into a maintenance area filled with coiled pipework and several generators that thrummed in the space. Once in the compartment, they were able to stand and assess their surroundings.

In the steel walls above the pipes was a series of openings, each with a circular grill. There was a ladder giving access to a gallery platform that served all the vents. Dan counted five grills in all; five ways into the unknown.

"Which one?" he said.

"Middle one leads to the main hangar," Elspeth said.

"Is this you or Johns, now?"

"It's Johns but through me," she said, hoping to give him some reassurance she was still his colleague.

"Is there a ship we can use to get out of here?" he asked hopefully.

"There is but that's not why we're going there."

He was suddenly looking at her. "Care to elaborate? Or is this *Show and Tell*?"

She held up a hand and tilted her head as if listening. "The people we need to meet will be in the hangar. We have to help them."

"You mean they're there now?"

"No." She paused, then continued. "But they'll be there soon. Events are moving fast."

"You don't seem sure." Dan wasn't surprised. He wasn't sure either.

"I'm just getting used to how this works, that's all." She wrinkled her nose, putting lines on her otherwise unblemished face. "This stuff is coming third hand. It's like trying to remember something important when you've got a bad dose of the flu. Apparently, it becomes easier with time."

Dan moved towards the ducts. "We don't have a lot of time, Elspeth. God knows what these fuckers are planning to do with our planet."

"Careful, Dan. You're showing signs of actually giving a shit," she said, smiling.

"It's early days," he said, returning her grin.

A scuffling, scraping sound came from behind Elspeth and Dan's grin tumbled from his face as she saw him look over her shoulder.

"Elspeth, get down!"

To make sure she complied, Dan grabbed hold of her lapels with one, great hand and yanked her to the floor.

Seconds later, an arc-blast turned Dan's face to flame.

***

His hands and face smarting with heat, Bart rolled across the platform. Just before the conflagration had melted metal and flesh in a bizarre silent and spectacular flash of light, he'd turned his head so as not to blind himself.

The aliens were not so lucky. The causeway was gone, the explosion had severed the infrastructure from the main platform, sending the whole walkway into the abyss. The shockwave had also sent twisted, burning shapes all around Bart, and he recognised them as the remnants of the creatures who had been firing upon him only moments earlier. Within the flames, the bodies hissed and spat fat, giving off a greasy stink that had Bart heaving in disgust.

He climbed to his feet, wiping bile from his chin, stunned by what had just happened, still trying to dissociate from an act of wanton destruction dealt by his own hand.

Taking an unsteady step, he tried to establish the best way forward. There were four causeways still available to him, but one he'd already exhausted, and there was no way he was going back to the lake and the hideous creature that lurked there.

He tried to be positive, falling back on his intrinsic nature, pushing on as though his sense of purpose hadn't taken a hit. It was a tough call; all the scenarios were clouded with the events of recent times. He drew upon thoughts of his parents, the way they would press on, undaunted by the adversity life would throw at them.

His father's voice was in his mind. "Keep your mind on today, yesterday has already had its glory."

It was the same with moments, Bart now found. Shelving those that had passed by, seeking out new opportunities, but his goal remained the same: to find a craft to take him to civilisation where he could raise the alarm. He made for the nearest causeway, not sure of what lay ahead but determined to strive for escape.

What about the others? his mind said, the accusation stalling his steps. *Are you going to just leave them behind, leave them to the kind of terrible fate that befell Collins?*

To kickstart the debate, he applied scientific reasoning. By getting out of there he'd be able to summon help, the kind of help that would be more effective in saving his colleagues. There would also be a delay, begging the question: would any surviving members of his team sustain their wellbeing while he was summoning any kind of rescue?

There was also the small question of: *were* there any team members left to save?

Bart couldn't ignore the final aspect to all this and *that* was the ethical dilemma. He knew these invaders posed a threat to Earth and all life forms who flourished here. Beneficence - the needs of the many over that of the individual - was a strong tenet, and he knew it.

He thought about this, the realisation that he may never find the means to escape taking precedent in his thoughts, becoming more real. He took in a breath, his conclusion now solidified. He would not look for a means to escape, he would find a way to destroy this entire complex and eliminate the existential threat to his planet, to his family and the billions of families like them all around the world.

With a heavy heart, Bart shouldered the burden as he would a rucksack, and made his way to the causeway, navigating past blossoming pools of flame. As he moved, he could hear the platform creak, and under his feet vibrations sent warning messages that the explosion had caused more structural damage than he'd first thought.

He quickened his pace, eager to be free of the platform, and get going down the gangway before the infrastructure collapsed. There were hog-squeals as metal protested at his movement, something fell, clattering against the wall as it disappeared into the gloom below.

Bart clutched at the cylindrical handrails either side of the gangway, trying to keep steady as the whole structure shimmied ahead of him, disorientating his eye-line. He held his breath and increased speed, sensing that time was waning, the death knell well and truly ringing for the platform and its tributaries.

The walkway protested at his movement, but he pressed on regardless. He could see a small grid in the distance, railings providing a perimeter as a run of skeletal, metal steps headed both up to the heavens and, much to Bart's delight, downwards.

The causeway began shaking, the sudden movement throwing Bart to the grilled floor, scuffing his knees and hands. Something whipped past him, a thick cable securing the handrails to the walls snapping under severe torque. Panicked, he scrambled to his feet and charged onwards, moving ever closer to the gallery platform.

A huge groan came from somewhere behind him, several thwacking sounds filled his ears, the hiss of cables cutting through the space. He felt the floor beneath him dropping away and jumped, arms outstretched, reaching desperately for the gallery handrail.

A cable came lashing through the murk, taking off his hands at the wrists, as though he was already a ghost, lacking any substance, the pain putting a scream into his throat, a scream that he took with him all the way down to the cavern floor.

The platform followed a few seconds later.

CHAPTER FIFTEEN

Knowles sat staring at Olok through the observation window. Her mind was racing as she tried to establish the alien scientist's angle, the ruse that he'd established to get her to comply.

"That's bullshit. How can I be pregnant?"

"Well, let us just say it did not – at any point during the process – involve the term 'fuck'," Olok mused. His assistants giggled like excited toddlers through a speaker grill.

As Knowles digested his words, she remembered the dull ache in her abdomen. Again, her hands went to the spot and she ruffled the gown, the crackling noise rising as she agitated the material.

"What did you do?" she whispered, a knot in her stomach joined in with the chaos going on in her belly.

"What your kind would refer to as IVF. A simple procedure, yeti semen and your ovaries, and some - how should I put it - ah, yes, some *scientific encouragement*, of course. This is not a natural symbiotic procedure, after all. But our technology was able to unite that which ordinarily would be incompatible."

She went over to Sully and looked down upon his inert form. There were tears falling from his eyes, moistening the headrest. Knowles placed a hand upon his brow, her fingers gentle, protective.

Olok spoke through the speaker and in his voice, Knowles could hear not only victory but wonder.

"And what we see now is the key to it all. The *connection* that is not crude like that of hybrids. But emotional harmony; just think of how that would blossom in the mutual love for a child. The solidarity of parents and the most precious gift they could give to the universe. The child will be a 'unique entity', a contract fulfilled."

Knowles rounded on him. "You're fucking monsters."

Olok continued, undeterred by her insult. "Yet through monstrosity there is also creation. And the opportunity for you to rid your world of our presence. Do you have such nobility within you?"

"*If* this works -"

"It has a high scientific probability. It will work." Olok was stern in his conviction.

"*If* this works, what do these clients want with this *unique entity?*"

"Well, as far as I know, that is outside the scope of the contract agreement, so I would have to say, *who cares.*"

Knowles' anger was bright. "I care. Sully cares. Why would we hand over our child without knowing what will happen to it?"

"To set your planet free. But if you really want to know, I can only surmise."

"Then do it." She gritted her teeth. Her desire to end this infernal creature was so great it made her limbs twitch with fury.

Olok tilted his head. "They are known only as *Sanctum* and as a race have an affinity for cosmic faith, so it may have something to do with their deeply held religious beliefs. They are very secretive, which is why this contract was worth so much to our people."

"Sanctum?" Knowles said.

"Well that's as close as our translation system allows for your language. But enough, Knowles. It's time to decide on how we proceed. Will you concede and come with us, or will things have to become unpleasant and we take you anyway?"

Knowles turned to her companion, still secured to his bed. "What you think, big fella?"

Sully blinked away his tears and nodded.

She bowed her head. "Yeah. Me too."

Olok twisted his snout into a strained smile and turned to his assistants. "Prep the shuttle. We leave in one rotation."

"Hey!" Knowles' shout came through the grill, startling him.

"What is it?" Olok replied briskly.

Knowles' gaze was steel as she pointed to her gown. "Get me my fucking clothes."

***

His bulky body bristling with irritation, Druh marched through the corridors leading to the main control centre. At one time, the central pod would have been the ship's bridge, a place of silver alloy and purple titanium, from which their scientific cruiser slipped through time and space in search of methods to fulfil the contracts considered the purpose of their species.

He was, of course, already planning a contingency report, and in this report he would be suggesting that the Chief Scientist had actively encouraged the human incursion, seeing a new avenue of exploration that may achieve their contractual goals. Given Olok's renown for recklessness, no one was going to question any document stating this lie as fact.

To support his statement, Druh would be using solid evidence. He'd already been briefed on an explosion on a maintenance causeway in sector eight that had killed fifteen guards and put two elevators out of commission, and humans were reportedly involved in this incident. This was on top of the flood in chamber five and two hybrids having to be euthanised.

Now there were testimonies coming through that Olok had captured the human and the snow beast, and currently had them detained in his lab. The actions of his Chief Scientist were proving somewhat unnerving, dare he say, even by usual standards, reckless.

Up to a point, Druh could understand Olok's stance. Being away from family for so long, even with the nuances of quantum technology and stasis capabilities, had consequences on the mental prowess of those who were frustrated with being so far away from those they held dear.

The contempt for this ethic was made plain relatively early on in the scientific tour, begging Druh to question why Olok had ever taken the role of Chief Scientist. The answer always was, of course, the scientific challenge. Druh only hoped that Olok's genius would outdo his maverick actions, proving everyone wrong, and sealing the contract for one of the most clandestine races in the universe.

Yet, once again, Olok was skirting round the fringes of protocol. Olok had not maintained communication with Druh and this silence had the administrator highly suspicious.

A small crew of technicians stopped working on a section of wall where a panel had been removed to expose the machinery beneath. The ship was high maintenance, and Druh wasn't so sure that even after they had achieved their goal for Sanctum it would be able to make it back through the wormhole used to bring them so far from home.

No matter, there were other ways. It just meant it would take much longer and with no firm sense of direction. Hopefully, it wouldn't come to that and they would leave as they came, all those centuries ago. The machinery kept this place in stasis, they still had time manipulated and on their side.

It was all in the hands of Olok and the prospect didn't sit well with him. Druh walked into the control centre as several of its crew approached, eager to give updates. To prevent a garbled bombardment of facts, he held up his hand to silence them. They stood to attention, waiting for sanction to speak.

"Where is the Chief Scientist?" he asked.

The operatives looked at each other and then scanned the room as though they'd only just realised Olok was not amongst them.

"Who is from Olok's lab?" he demanded with exasperation.

A skinny grey arm shot into the air, long fingers wriggling like worms through dirt. "Me, Administrator Druh."

"An update, now."

"Olok asks me to report that it is done," the lab operative said proudly.

"And?" Druh said, crossing his arms expectantly.

"That is the message, Administrator." The operative was despondent, realising that he'd not given a good enough answer.

Druh screwed up his snout in annoyance. "I will go to the lab to see Olok for myself. We are not to be disturbed."

He went to turn on his heel and leave the control pod, his mood suddenly very upbeat. It seemed the wait could be almost over.

The lab operative's eyes turned yellow, the colour of uncertainty.

"What is it?" Druh said, his tone impatient.

"Olok is not in the lab, Administrator." The operative found something interesting to look at on the floor.

"Then where is he?" Druh snapped.

"The main hangar."

"And what is he doing in the main hangar?" Druh was clearly agitated now. What in the name of commerce was going on?

After a moment of hesitancy, the operative responded in a quiet voice. "He appears to be commissioning the shuttle."

Druh could not believe his hearing nodules.

Incredulous, he thumped a nearby chair, sending a briefing tablet skittering to the floor where it broke in two. "What? Get me a trans-tunnel buggy and the Watch Commander. Now!"

The operative ran off to a console to act out the administrator's orders, grateful that he no longer had to incur the contemptuous, red stare of his leader.

***

His face gone, Dan fell to the floor, his legs jittering as though they still wanted to be upright and getting out of there. Elspeth screamed in shock and anguish as she ducked behind the pipe work. Another slash of bright light cut through the gloom, this time puncturing a pipe and sending lurid green steam into the air.

The blast had come from the gully they'd just exited, the alien about to extricate itself from the gap clutching a rifle, the muzzle still glowing red with heat.

Elspeth aimed the pistol and thumbed the trigger, her action fluid and devoid of hesitation. Her shot struck the alien trooper in the shoulder, splashing its blood against the frame of the outlet in a beautiful fan shape. The trooper lost his rifle, and Elspeth stepped from her hiding place, walked calmly up to the struggling creature, and shot it through the right eye.

A coldness came over her and, somewhere inside, she mourned the person that was no longer there. This was war and the first casualty was not innocence as the adage went, but naivety that she could do this kind of work without emotional consequence.

The alien quivered and for a second, she thought he was still alive. A hand squeezed through the meagre gap left between the dead body and the gully frame. Another trooper was trying to shove its colleague out of the way. Elspeth stooped and put the pistol through the gap, firing several times, hearing the squeals of pain from the murk.

Stepping away, she shoved her pistol in her belt and retrieved the arc-rifle from the floor.

On her way to the ladder, she paused. Stooping beside her fallen comrade, she placed a comforting hand on Dan's chest, taking care not to look at the damage done to his face.

Her heart was heavy yet grateful to him for saving her life. His sacrifice was something she vowed to honour in the trials to come. Good people came in many different forms, sometimes who they really were beneath the personas they threw up against the ills of the world came to the surface just a little too late.

She wiped away a tear from her alabaster cheek. "Sleep well, Daniel Lake."

With those words, she headed off towards an even greater unknown.

***

Olok kept pace with Knowles. Ahead, the gurney glided through the air on autopilot, the shimmering restrictors still securing Sully to its steel frame. The corridor was alive with contrasting noises. The swish of Olok's tunic, the soft padding of Knowles' boots against the metal floor, and the static hum of the restrictors.

The sense of growing euphoria had Olok feeling as though he could join the gurney and dance on the air. His achievement was staggering; the implications for the future beyond measure. Soon he would be on the shuttle and leaving this miserable existence. The reluctant Knowles and the yeti savage would be held in stasis, to prevent their meddling while in transit.

As he'd said to Knowles, the science was sound, but he still needed them in case anything unforeseen occurred and they needed to start the insemination process again. All he was required to do was get his precious cargo on board before Druh began complicating matters with his bluster.

They made their way from the lab and down an access channel that dipped for a while before a slope brought them up into a great hangar.

The human was behaving, the squad of armed guards was making sure of that, and the beast was secure. Olok doubted that the restraints would be removed until the creature was placed in the shuttle's brig, if at all. He figured if Knowles remained compliant then so would her furry companion. He ran it through his mind a few times and liked how the maths worked out.

In the hangar, a sleek silver rocket-ship glimmered under overhead arc-lamps, its nose aimed at a set of huge, arched doors, several hundred yards away. The shuttle was capable of the kind of speeds that would have Earth scientists dribbling, easily able to navigate the wormholes of the universe. If not, then he knew enough spaceports where he could hire another ship that would meet his needs. All he needed to do was get off-world and make it safely to the stars.

The guards fanned out as they moved through the docking space. Scattered about them were a series of maintenance lockers and storage crates. Cylindrical fuel cells were sunk into the deck at intervals, their surfaces striped ebony and silver. The hangar was supported by smooth struts that rose either side of the bulkhead, the rivets formed large metal domes that glittered like stardust.

Approaching the craft, Olok saw a figure alighting from the steps that dropped from the underbelly. He recognised the shuttle's captain and acknowledged him with a wave of a hand.

"Is everything in order, Captain Shirak?"

"I have instructions to hold boarding until Administrator Druh arrives," Shirak barked as he adjusted his flight suit.

Olok could not hide his frustration. "Then at least stow our assets in the brig."

"No one is to board, Olok. My brief is clear."

Before Olok could protest, there was a steadily growing hum on the air and Administrator Druh emerged from the ramp on a bulky transportation buggy. He was accompanied by the station Watch Commander. The driver pulled up next to Olok and the Administrator's face was stern.

"Ah, Chief Scientist," Druh crooned. "I believe you have an update for me."

CHAPTER SIXTEEN

The atmosphere in the hangar was awkward and bristling with tension. With not a little effort, Druh disembarked from the transport buggy. The Watch Commander alighted with him, catching up with him easily as the Administrator waddled over to Olok.

Druh's huge eyes took in the sight of Sully and Knowles en route, the huge irises crimson with anger.

He stood before his troublesome Chief Scientist. "Well, Olok? Explain yourself."

Olok's arrogance turned his words to a bored sneer. "I have delivered my report, Administrator. And made clear my intention."

"Your 'report' was at best ambiguous and delivered verbally by a lab-operative," Druh said. "And this is why you are standing outside the shuttle and not boarding it."

"We have achieved our aim, Druh." In frustration, Olok rubbed fervently at his generous forehead. "Let us fulfil our contractual duty and be done with this place."

Druh eyed Knowles suspiciously. "I would ask you to come and discuss the future of our place on this world in private, Olok."

Knowles stepped in. Her irritation was evident as she spoke through gritted teeth. "You've got no place on this world. I made a deal."

"Whatever agreement you have with our Chief Scientist has not been sanctioned by me or anyone with the authority to make it binding," Druh said, looking directly at Olok.

"You saying this deal is off?" Knowles said, her anger now coating her words.

"No, he is *not*," Olok snapped.

Ignoring Olok, Druh turned to Knowles. "There is no *contract* for this agreement and therefore it cannot be endorsed at this time. There needs to be caveats in place, and the legalities addressed."

Knowles laughed in disbelief. "Legalities? Are you for fucking real? The deal is that we go with him. And you leave this planet for good."

The Administrator nodded his head as if this all made sense. "Well, that is *exactly* what I am talking about. We cannot leave this planet. There is too much investment tied up with it. Olok had no right to propose such a thing."

"It was a ruse, Druh. To get them to leave amicably," Olok lied.

"You bastard," Knowles said. Her sentiment was echoed by Sully who gave out a loud roar and began rocking on the gurney.

"Stop that," Olok snapped. He stepped up and lifted a hand. Between his fingers was a small, square box with a funnel and a single red button, which he depressed. The restrictors turned a fiery orange and Sully cried out in pain.

Knowles went to rush at Olok but was stopped by several arc-rifles brought up into her face. An alien hand slapped down on her shoulder, holding her still.

Olok released the button and Sully whimpered in relief. Knowles clenched her hands in fury, her eyes never leaving the scientist.

Druh broke the stalemate. "The human and the beast will be returned to the lab until we can establish contractual arrangements with our superiors. Then, we shall proceed with the transport. But it will be I, not our Chief Scientist, who will deliver the product. Are we clear, Captain Shirak?"

Shirak thumped his chest in a smart salute.

"That is an outrage!" Olok screamed. "This is all my work. You have a duty, Druh."

Druh puffed out his ample upper body. "You have failed to comply with any regulations, Olok. Your recklessness has put this operation in jeopardy, therefore your rights as Chief Scientist are rescinded. I wanted to do this in private, and with dignity, but you have left me no option. Do not make me embarrass you further. You will hand over your research to my security staff and you will assist as a lab-operative until punishment is sanctioned by our superiors. But let us be clear, you are destined to remain here at this base indefinitely."

"No!" Olok stomped around the hangar, this puerile act making Knowles laugh despite the bizarre situation going on about her.

"Mock me at your peril, human," he shrieked, activating the box still in his hand. Sully writhed on the gurney, his cries mixing with Olok's mocking laughter.

It was Druh who attempted to intervene. "Enough of this madness, Olok. Release him and step down."

But Olok ignored his superior and Knowles noticed that the guards were becoming nervous, their weapons lowering, unsure of what was going on.

"Instructions, Administrator?" the Watch Commander said above the din.

"Restrain Olok," Druh instructed.

The Watch Commander addressed his troopers. "Secure that subjugation device. Arrest Olok."

Three troopers attended to the order, grabbing Olok and yanking the box free of his hand, making him spit with fury. Sully passed out on the gurney, and Knowles' hatred for the ex-Chief Scientist boiled in her chest.

But, as Olok wrestled with the troops, their comrades were distracted enough by the commotion to give Knowles her moment. She bent an elbow and drove it into the stomach of the nearest guard, doubling him up, and then yanked an arc-pistol from his belt holster as he collapsed. She came up, putting down two nearby troopers with shots to the head and chest, sending everyone else running for cover.

She grabbed the gurney and ran headlong towards the access ramp, letting it go as several arc-rifles sent bolts into the suspension mechanism, shattering it. Without its anti-gravitational system, the gurney tipped, Sully still pinned to it and three more blasts hit the exposed underside as it landed, blasting apart the restrictor apparatus tethered to the base. Suddenly free, Sully rolled away, pinned down by an intense barrage coming from across the hangar. Knowles used the gurney for cover, the forest of sparks thrown up all around her.

Hiding behind the transport buggy, Olok glowered at Druh. "This is where your interference has got us. Tell them to stop shooting. We cannot risk our assets."

"All of this changes nothing, Olok. Your time as Chief Scientist is at an end, no matter what happens next," Druh panted.

"Then it is truly up to me to save the contract." Olok pulled a pistol from the folds of his cloak. He put three shots into the Administrator without hesitating. Beside him, Captain Shirak looked aghast.

"Sorry, Captain, but this way it is a lot easier to sustain the deceit." Shirak's head disintegrated as Olok fired at close range.

Jumping to his feet, Olok ran towards the shuttle. With the troopers occupied with their firefight, there was no one to stop him. He entered the shuttle, shot down the two crew members hiding inside, and withdrew the ramp.

Several moments later, the sound of arc-weaponry was drowned out by the roar of engines.

***

Elspeth sniffed back tears and, leaving Dan's body behind, raised the rifle. She blasted out the grill above her. Mounting the ladder, she took comfort in her mind-cafe, where Johns told her exactly what route to take.

The ventilation shaft was a corrugated pipe, eight feet in diameter, and a warm wind whooshed through it, sending Elspeth's fiery, red hair out in tendrils, ruffling her clothes as though the material was being tugged by many unseen hands. She was at least able to walk upright, the arc-rifle ready to blast anything that appeared unfriendly.

Johns' thoughts were not fluid, they were operating as though on a live feed, updates happening in real time, as her will commanded. Elspeth would be asked to pause as her disembodied associate played catch up on whatever events were happening elsewhere, and then relayed them to her consciousness.

It was an odd sensation because these messages came through as her own thoughts. She knew the way to the hangar, she knew what actors were in play in this event, but her primary focus was that of a woman called Clarice Knowles and a yeti named Sully. They were all part of the psychic soup in which Johns dipped his mind and fed Elspeth what was needed to sustain her safety.

Ahead, there were tributaries, three pipes that fanned out, each stretching off beyond what her eyes could see. Johns told her to go left. Before doing so, she checked behind her to make sure she wasn't being followed. The conduit was clear, and she continued.

She'd walked three hundred yards when the unmistakable sound of distant arc-weapons crackled through the pipe. There were tiny flashes from up ahead and, resisting the urge to turn tail, she ran towards the firefight.

Coming to another grill, she peered through. Below there was the hangar, and bright arc-blasts were streaking from right to left, plumes of bright flame repeatedly erupted against the bulkhead. Squinting against the brightness, she saw a black woman and a large, fur-clad figure keeping low behind an arched strut.

Instantly, she knew she'd found Knowles and Sully. Now all she had to do was find a way to get them out of there.

Without getting everyone killed in the process.

***

From her vantage point, Knowles looked on helplessly as the silver rocket-ship lifted from the deck. She questioned why Olok was so keen to abandon them, given the investment he'd put into getting them off Earth. The ship hovered and then skimmed across the hangar, disappearing at ridiculous speed, and without a slipstream, through the hangar exit.

Knowles looked at the buggy and saw splashes of goo oozing from the wheels. Alien blood. *Jesus*, she thought, *the guy's gone and topped his boss. How's that for breach of contract?*

Sully put an arm on hers. "Trapped," he said.

"Got to think of a way out of here," she said.

Knowles looked at the slope leading out of the hangar. She gauged it was only ten feet away, but ten feet of open space, no cover at all. The opposite direction was the buggy, same distance but with the struts of a loading bay in between. Although she was anxious to get out of there, she still wanted to get out of there in one piece.

"We might need to go backwards to get forwards, Sully," she said, pointing at the struts. He gave a thumbs up.

Knowles nodded. "On three," she muttered. "One, two ..."

They moved, Sully hefting the gurney, his hands placed on the top and bottom edge, swinging it vertically, and placing his face against the underside. With Knowles behind him, they shuffled backwards, the gurney shielding them both, the metal surface deflecting arc-blasts, sending them ricocheting through the hangar.

Knowles felt an arc-bolt singe her hair; the ensuing explosion as it slapped into the wall next to her sent hot sparks onto her neck and the yelled in pain. Sully was suddenly lifting her, propelling her towards the bulkhead, and they ducked behind the struts as more detonations flared about them. Sully put out a smouldering patch on his arm as he discarded the gurney.

"This is not good," Knowles said. "But it's better than where we were."

She observed the buggy. Two bodies lay behind it, one missing a head. She recognised the figure of the Administrator who had tried to clip Olok's wings, arc-burns on his chest.

More explosions, another salvo of arc-weapons pouring their searing, scorching heat into bulkheads and struts. Knowles and Sully hunkered down under a deluge of sputtering sparks.

"Shit! We're pinned down like a second-rate pro-wrestler," Knowles shouted.

Sully seemed intent on staring at the buggy, his dark eyes reflecting the sparks and arc-rifle blasts. Knowles was about to ask him what his plan was when, without warning or explanation, he left the safety of cover and charged at the buggy.

"Sully! What the hell?"

Left with no choice, Knowles ducked out from behind the strut and laid down covering fire. The arc-pistol was pitiful against the rows of rifles spitting fire across the bay, a slingshot against missiles.

Her intervention held the squad on the left at bay, but another burst of arc-blasts came from those on the right, the gurney taking several hits, as well as the bulkhead. The barrage forced Knowles back into hiding, with a torrent of curses.

Something else was added to the mix – another arc-blast coming from a vent above the hangar bay, slaying two troopers on the right before they realised what was happening.

Three troopers were directed by their Watch Commander to exchange fire, bolts flying towards the vent where Knowles could make out the image of a woman with red hair ducking back inside the conduit for cover as explosions riddled the frame.

Opening fire again, Knowles felt a sense of relief. "No idea who you are lady but thank fuck you're here."

Meanwhile, Sully quickly covered the distance between strut and buggy, his powerful limbs thumping on the deck, trampling the bodies of Druh and Captain Shirak. He went low, turning his shoulder, and slammed into the buggy, dead centre. There was a dull thud and the vehicle flipped and rolled. The momentum sent it cartwheeling through the hangar, each bounce giving out firefly sparkles as it made contact with the deck.

The troopers were hesitant as they watched this incredible sight, this wonder of implausible strength. The buggy's chassis began to come apart, metal flying, the debris making the troops huddle down behind the crates and storage lockers.

Through this confusion, Sully had not stayed still. The yeti veered towards the group on the left and was amongst them before any realised he was there. He swatted the Watch Commander across the head, caving in his face. He used the smashed body to beat two others to death in a brutal frenzy.

Preoccupied with the carnage across the hangar, the troopers on the right repositioned themselves to take down Sully, allowing Knowles the opportunity to break cover and open fire on them. She'd hit three before panic set in with the others, and they were forced to defend their position.

Knowles saw more arc-blasts from above; the red-headed sniper was back in the fray. Another trooper went down, an arm missing at the shoulder.

By this time, Sully was finished with his assault, his fur dripping with alien blood. He rose from behind the storage lockers with an arc-rifle in each hand, sending blasts across the hangar, slicing into the troopers, driving them out into the sights of Knowles and Elspeth who slaughtered them with clinical proficiency.

In the silence that followed, Knowles ran across the hangar to Sully, throwing her arms about him as best she could. He hugged her gently.

They heard footfalls and both turned, rifles ready. Elspeth held up an empty hand in a peaceful gesture.

"Hey, I'm on your side," she said with a nervous smile.

"We'll see," Knowles replied, her weapon still raised.

CHAPTER SEVENTEEN

At the helm of the shuttle, Olok simmered, his rage kept under control only by his determination to action his contingency plan. Druh had talked about the containment protocol before, but what Olok had in mind was something a little more radical. Prompting this was, of course, the fact he'd murdered two of his work colleagues, a predicament from which there was no going back without some serious story amendments. Plus, there was making sure he acted fast enough to protect his assets from those numbskull guards.

There were two parts to his plan, and one did involve the use of the containment protocol. The second factored in the Disaster Management Initiative (DMI), and this was perhaps where things became controversial. The DMI involved erasing all evidence of their existence on the planet below. The substance known as *quicksilver* that ran as glittering veins throughout the caverns and caves, giving light in the darkness, would ultimately be used to purge their presence, their existence, on the planet.

Such was the nature of DMI, its existence was only known by the Administrator and the Chief Scientist. Once activated, the quicksilver would ignite in a phased, controlled burn, its volatile chemical properties interacting with any alien organism on a quantum level, collapsing atoms, sucking them out of existence.

When all was said and done, quicksilver was an ultra-efficient means of sterilising a site, without any recourse.

If, of course, you discounted the small matter of mass murder.

There was another downside to Olok's plan. Once the alien infrastructure was erased, the silver veins would disappear and leave a fissure, this fissure would then collapse, undermining everything above and below, along with the mountain's integrity. The danger to Knowles and Sully was a very real risk, although Olok, and his brilliant, yet cruel mind factored this into his survival model.

He'd make sure the hangar he'd just left behind was the last zone to ignite, giving his precious assets time to get out. Then he would keep them trapped using the containment protocol, the shield of nanoflies in the stratosphere putting the entire planet in a stasis field.

There was a small matter of blocking out UV light and the potential ice age that would ensue while the stasis field was in place. But that was a trifle compared to losing Knowles and Sully. He could only go back to his world successful; it would offset what had been done here. He'd have to return here after a time, hide out in a nearby star system, recruit a team to return and retrieve Knowles *et al*. He felt confident his strategy was viable, with a strong success outcome.

The shuttle accelerated through the clouds, punching through the stratosphere. Once out of orbit, Olok hastily set his plan in motion.

***

"Who are you?" Knowles said, her voice heavy with suspicion.

"Name's Elspeth. I'm from Appleby's rescue team."

Knowles bristled. "Appleby is dead. And he wasn't any friend of mine."

Elspeth gave out a sad smile. "I get that, I really do. But things are bigger than this now. There's no sides, just humans sticking together."

"There's more than just humans," Knowles said, leaning into Sully.

In a conciliatory move, Elspeth dropped her arc-rifle to the deck. "I hear you. But please, trust me. Things are about to get pretty weird."

"Fuck me," Knowles said, but lowered her weapon. "Now *that's* a claim."

"Yeah. We need to leave here, now."

"We're kinda trying, lady."

"The ship that's just taken off, it's not done. There's a contingency plan – a containment protocol - to hold the world in stasis until the creature on it can return," Elspeth said, the haste in her voice making her sound desperate.

"Return for who?"

"You two."

Knowles' rifle came up again. "You know a hell of a lot about this, maybe too much for you to be coming any closer."

Elspeth's face became stern, but despite this, a tear fell down her left cheek. "I know a damn sight more. And I'll tell you everything. But we must get out of here, away from this hangar, this base."

Knowles shook her head. "I'm not going anywhere with you."

More tears now, the frustration boiling over like a geyser. "Look, if I'd wanted you dead, would I have intervened just now?"

"She has point," Sully said unexpectedly.

Knowles scowled at him. "*Now* you want to say something?"

Elspeth took a step forward. "Please, Clarice. If you want to live, we have to go."

"And if *you* want to live, don't ever call me Clarice again."

In the distance, Knowles heard many dull thumps, breaking the impasse. Then, the ground began to tremble.

Knowles looked down at her boots. "Now what?"

Elspeth looked about her. "You know that containment protocol I was talking about? That's how it starts."

An unseen explosion buckled the wall surrounding the vent, the galley platform going from horizontal to zigzag in a second of intense pressure. Another quickly followed and this time the metal tore open in several places, and tendrils of brilliant white light crawled through them like probing fingers, searching. Searching.

Lightning bolt ferocity followed, sending the three of them running for shelter. Electricity arced through the hangar, but the spectacular light targeted only the fallen alien bodies, wrapping around them, lifting them clear of the ground. In mid-air the corpses were cocooned, multiple lariats of light that crackled and fizzed.

"What the fuck?" Knowles hollered over the din.

"They're destroying the evidence," Elspeth said. "Wiping out their existence."

Knowles watched the fading spectacle with glee. "If it means all these fuckers are dead and gone for good then I'm not complaining."

The tendrils faded, leaving nothing of the aliens consumed by them. Deep within the alien structure, more explosions could be heard, and other sounds too, screams of those being erased while still alive.

The hangar started to shudder, the deck shimmying like an old school carnival Shake Shack. Metal plates lifted, thick stalagmites punching through.

"So what do you want to do, Knowles? It's your call," Elspeth shouted. "But I'm getting out of here, either way."

"I guess now we can say we're on the same side," Knowles grinned.

They all clambered to their feet and began running, Elspeth slightly ahead of her new-found companions. She felt her stomach lurch as she fell, a scream in her throat as she saw a gaping hole open beneath her.

Sully scooped her out of free fall, pulling her away from the crater.

Overhead, the lights and bulkheads buckled, dropping to the deck, clattering, or smashing, sending shards of glass and metal in all directions. One of the far walls gave way and huge seams of rock smashed through, knocking aside a fuel cell, the explosion loud, making their ears ring. The conflagration added to the chaos, hell had come to the place and there appeared little chance of escape, but Knowles sensed Olok would never have destroyed this place and risk compromising her.

She looked across to the hangar doors, still thrown wide, and the white snowscape a brilliant backdrop.

They could make it, she knew it.

"Hangar doors! Come on!"

They ran as one, bunched together, urging each other on as debris rained down about them, blasts and booms rocking the whole structure, driving them along, the brisk wind as they neared the huge bay doors clearing away the stink of smoke, rousing them.

Clambering over the metal skirt and tumbling into the snow, they each crawled through the freezing ground.

With a final groan, the roof of the hangar collapsed, flame and dust belching out onto the plateau where it was ripped to nothing by the wind.

***

In the upper atmosphere, trillions of nanoflies covered the Earth like an invisible net. They held orbit, dormant ghosts, humanity ignorant to their existence.

Once Olok activated the DMI, thus ensuring the base in the snow was wiped clean of his exploits, he called upon the nanoflies to wake from their centuries-old slumber. Just as they had existed up to now, so the invisible army exacted their influence behind a shield of anonymity. The only hint to those below that things were awry was the purple hue that clouded the atmosphere.

Satellites were sabotaged by a co-ordinated electro-magnetic pulse, the ISS robbed of power, the crew freezing to death before they could suffocate. The Earth was to suffer its fate alone, an unknown entity to almost everyone, save for the Chief Scientist who at that point was setting course for a small star system only three light years away. He would be docking on the first civilised planet by the time the first snowstorm turned the Earth to ice. He had longer to patiently plan for the time to return.

The world he'd left behind was a prison and he was its gaoler.

***

Leaving the fractured base behind them, Sully led the way, his ever-faithful snout seeking out a refuge in the air. Knowles and Elspeth clung to him for warmth, each comforted by a great arm. Still, their teeth chattered, and the skin of their exposed faces were numb with cold.

The massif was silent, the air brimming with a stillness that left them all with a pressing sense of foreboding. They made their way back down the mountain, navigating rocks and ice, Sully lifting them where the landscape became too difficult or hazardous to circumvent.

A low rumble came from overhead, causing Knowles to look skyward. Multiple streaks of light seared the darkening sky, like many, many comets passing by.

"What the hell is that?" she said.

Elspeth made an assessment via Johns. "It's the International Space Station breaking up in the atmosphere."

"Jesus."

Pressing on, they moved west for a few hundred metres and Elspeth recognised the yellow pool she and Dan had used to descend into the alien labyrinth. The thought of her companion, and his ultimate end, made her feel melancholy, and she allowed Sully's warmth to permeate, trying to draw some comfort.

A bloody streak guided them to the body of Chris, and Knowles looked across at Elspeth, who was now giving in to her grief and softly crying into Sully's side. She reached across and took hold of the weeping woman's hand, holding it tightly.

Onwards they went, observing the mangled remnants of the helicopter's tail fin, and the huge hole into which the fuselage had been swallowed. At that point, Sully guided them north and Knowles saw the familiar rocky wall that had provided them with shelter during the blizzard.

A dull thud put a small explosion of snow ahead and she half expected an alien war machine to appear from the cave entrance. Another eruption, this time to her left, then another to her right.

"Oh my god, look, look!" Elspeth gasped.

Birds, hundreds of them, were falling like rain. Each one frozen in mid-flight. The three of them ducked inside the confines of the cave, shutting out the terrible reality falling from the skies.

Knowles scanned the massif as it lay littered with avian corpses.

"That alien fucker is killing the world," she muttered. "And there's fuck all we can do about it."

EPILOGUE

Inside the cave, Knowles could feel the heat radiating out from the tunnels deep below.

"Seems we got kickback from all the chaos," she said, placing a hand on warm rock. "Might last, might not."

"It'll last," Elspeth said, knowingly. Johns was still with her, a strange kind of assurance in these uncertain times.

They stood on the threshold, facing outside as a low rumble of thunder rolled across the valley. The clouds billowing high in the atmosphere had a sinister purple tinge, sucking the light from the sky. Soon everyone in the world would be exposed, and there was no way of stopping it.

Elspeth looked out at the oncoming storm. "We have a plan?"

Knowles leaned into Sully; hands placed on her abdomen.

"We survive," she said.

"And then?"

Knowles looked up at the sky as it was swallowed by the purple haze. But it was Sully who answered.

"We get even," he growled.

END

CHECK OUT OTHER GREAT BIGFOOT NOVELS

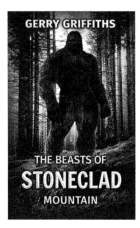

THE BEASTS OF STONECLAD MOUNTAIN
by **Gerry Griffiths**

Clay Morgan is overjoyed when he is offered a place to live in a remote wilderness at the base of a notorious mountain. Locals say there are Bigfoot living high up in the dense mountainous forest. Clay is skeptic at first and thinks it's nothing more than tall tales.

But soon Clay becomes a believer when giant creatures invade his new home and snatch his baby boy, Casey.

Now, Clay and his wife, Mia, must rescue their son with the help of Clay's uncle and his dog, a journey up the foreboding mountain that will take them into an unimaginable world...straight into hell!

BIGFOOT AWAKENED
by **Alex Laybourne**

A weekend away with friends was supposed to be fun. One last chance for Jamie to blow off some steam before she leaves for college, but when the group make a wrong turn, fun is the last thing they find.

From the moment they pass through a small rural town they are being hunted by whatever abominations live in the woods.

Yet, as the beasts attack and the truth is revealed, they learn that despite everything, man still remains the most terrifying evil of them all.

CHECK OUT OTHER GREAT CRYPTID NOVELS

SWAMP MONSTER MASSACRE
by **Hunter Shea**

The swamp belongs to them. Humans are only prey. Deep in the overgrown swamps of Florida, where humans rarely dare to enter, lives a race of creatures long thought to be only the stuff of legend. They walk upright but are stronger, taller and more brutal than any man. And when a small boat of tourists, held captive by a fleeing criminal, accidentally kills one of the swamp dwellers' young, the creatures are filled with a terrifyingly human emotion—a merciless lust for vengeance that will paint the trees red with blood.

TERROR MOUNTAIN
by **Gerry Griffiths**

When Marcus Pike inherits his grandfather's farm and moves his family out to the country, he has no idea there's an unholy terror running rampant about the mountainous farming community. Sheriff Avery Anderson has seen the heinous carnage and the mutilated bodies. He's also seen the giant footprints left in the snow—Bigfoot tracks. Meanwhile, Cole Wagner, and his wife, Kate, are prospecting their gold claim farther up the valley, unaware of the impending dangers lurking in the woods as an early winter storm sets in. Soon the snowy countryside will run red with blood on TERROR MOUNTAIN.

CHECK OUT OTHER GREAT CRYPTID NOVELS

BIGFOOT WAR
by Eric S. Brown

Now a feature film from Origin Releasing. For the first time ever, all three core books of the Bigfoot War series have been collected into a single tome of Sasquatch Apocalypse horror. Remastered and reedited this book chronicles the original war between man and beast from the initial battles in Babblecreek through the apocalypse to the wastelands of a dark future world where Sasquatch reigns supreme and mankind struggles to survive. If you think you've experienced Bigfoot Horror before, think again. Bigfoot War sets the bar for the genre and will leave you praying that you never have to go into the woods again.

CRYPTID ZOO
by Gerry Griffiths

As a child, rare and unusual animals, especially cryptid creatures, always fascinated Carter Wilde.

Now that he's an eccentric billionaire and runs the largest conglomerate of high-tech companies all over the world, he can finally achieve his wildest dream of building the most incredible theme park ever conceived on the planet...CRYPTID ZOO.

Even though there have been apparent problems with the project, Wilde still decides to send some of his marketing employees and their families on a forced vacation to assess the theme park in preparation for Opening Day.

Nick Wells and his family are some of those chosen and are about to embark on what will become the most terror-filled weekend of their lives—praying they survive.

STEP RIGHT UP AND GET YOUR FREE PASS...

TO CRYPTID ZOO

Printed in Great Britain
by Amazon

41970028R00086